I0669204

SuperSiblings

Inspiring stories of enterprising siblings

Prachi Garg

Happy Reading!!

loads of wishes

Prachi Garg 〰✔

Srishti
PUBLISHERS & DISTRIBUTORS

SRISHTI PUBLISHERS & DISTRIBUTORS
Registered Office: N-16, C.R. Park
New Delhi – 110 019
Corporate Office: 212A, Peacock Lane
Shahpur Jat, New Delhi – 110 049
editorial@srishtipublishers.com

First published by
Srishti Publishers & Distributors in 2018

Dedicated to my siblings –
Himadri Garg and Anant Garg.

Acknowledgements

This book has been possible due to the enormous love and support that people have given to me. It was their constant support that kept me going and ensured that I should be able to deliver it on time. I would like to thank everyone for making the journey smooth for me.

Family members play a great role to make such accomplishments possible. In my case as well, this holds true. Each one of them has been instrumental and has been there when required, especially my parents who encouraged me to bring out the best and being my biggest critic.

Arup Bose from Srishti Publishers for his faith in my concept and agreeing to publish the same.

Stuti Sharma, my editor, who undertook the tedious task of going through my manuscript, editing it and coming out with exciting ideas.

All my friends who provided me with constant moral support to make this happen.

All the readers of *Superwomen* and *SuperCouples*, whose love inspired me to pen down *SuperSiblings*.

And finally, all the lovely siblings who took out time and shared their brilliant stories with me, so that I could share them with you all.

I hope all of you get inspired with their journeys and contribute to the progress of the nation.

Contents

Swapnil *(right) and* **Mayur** *(left) kick-started* **360Track** *to help parents and educational institutes to be on the same platform and communicate seamlessly with each other and thus efficiently contribute to a child's academic growth.*

The Horizon of Successful Bonds

360Track by Swapnil & Mayur

More than two decades ago, little Swapnil and Mayur were often found playing in some silent corners, away from the chaos of their peers. The brothers would be seen engaged in building something. It didn't matter whether they had games or equipment or tools or even someone to teach them the next steps. Even at that stage, the duo would build, construct and create from scratch. They had not been afraid to be wrong and to work till the mistakes became achievements. Even today, after all those years of learning and unlearning, the siblings are unafraid, innovative and resourceful about constructing the best out of what life gives them.

Both brothers have degrees in Engineering in Information Technology and Computer Science. Mayur also completed his certification in Cyber Law. Swapnil, the elder of the two siblings, only by a year, has a passion for education. He enjoys studying and spreading the same to eager learners across different platforms. A motivational speaker, visionary and a man of his words, Swapnil is known by all and sundry for being a leader and moving hearts and minds with the clarity in his thoughts and determination of his actions. It is his ideology that acts as the cement in the relation between the brothers.

As a young teenager, Mayur, younger of the two siblings, was immensely attracted to the subject of computer science. Along with studying it as a subject in school, Mayur started exploring the various languages in the world of computers and immersed himself in computer programming, strengthening his basic understanding and working upwards to build new and complicated programs to push his boundaries of knowledge and experience in the subject. During his pursuit his diploma in Computer Technology as a young programmer, Mayur had already started building software and hardware solutions along with a few of his friends for clients from different verticals. With his entrepreneurial skills and sincerity towards development in computer technology, the young engineer has established himself not only as a skilled developer but also as a dedicated professional. This trait reflects strongly in his personal life too, building his character as one which is committed and productive. If Swapnil is the cement of their relationship, Mayur is the brick that helps to build this relationship taller and stronger. Together, they become the depth and strength of a unit that can achieve anything they want. This is one of the most exquisite examples of symbiotic symphony in the world of enterprises. A major challenge that people face is the lack of one or the other element in managing their businesses. If one is creative, one may lack the entrepreneurial streak. If one is great with business development organization and operations, one may be too occupied to build on the product. It is thus only wise to partner up with complementary talents and expertise to build a venture holistically. However, this is much easier said than done. First of all, to find people who share the same passion and equation with you on your vision is a challenge. Secondly, to find cognizance with their talents is a result of multiple permutations and combinations that is a matter of hit or miss. But most importantly, and many who have learned the hard way would nod is vehement agreement, to find a partner in business who you can trust, be in sync with and fall back on unconditionally is a luxury that most entrepreneurs do not find. In such a scenario, it is more than obvious why Swapnil and Mayur, brothers by birth and friends by fortune, decided to become co-founders of their dream child. Not only do they complement each other in their skills and nature, but also trust and support each other incessantly, that makes for a classic formula for a perfect yet effortless relationship between the two.

Thus began the siblings' journey into the professional world as partners. With the experience that Mayur had gained working in freelance projects in different realms include software and hardware solutions, web-designing, digital marketing and other technical expertise related to computer technology. However, when taking on a more organized and scaled approach in an effort to form a structured work flow, Swapnil came in with his expertise of structural and operational strategies. This helped to build the selection and extent of services that their enterprise would provide. Eventually, with research, experience and logical validation, they summed up their core services as Digital Marketing, Website Development, Mobile App Development and Software Development. With their USP as being creativity in the technical solutions they provide along with incomparable client service, the brothers established their dream venture in the name of The Horizon Technologies, an IT & Digital Media firm, that officially came into operation in the year 2013.

Most enterprises work backwards with their finances and accumulate funds before rolling into operation. However, with the co-founders of The Horizon Technologies, the management of the initial funds was a challenge that came with a lot of struggle, valuable lessons and above all, a family bond that changed the definition of what it means to stick together in good times and bad.

"The beginning was an unbelievable series of struggles. When we first started out, we didn't have enough funds to manage our expenses. It was at this stage when our father helped us out by withdrawing money from his provident fund and investing it in our dream. You have no idea how that made us feel – proud, overwhelmed and indeed inspired!" Swapnil recollects with a beaming smile. It was this benign support from the family that pushed the brothers to start off. Although, it would take them a little time to kick start the momentum and start acquiring clients and begin receiving projects at a regular pace.

"When people look at businesses, they only witness the glory days, successful deals and the value of the brand in the relative market. Very few people understand the pressure of sustenance, challenges of regular expenditures or even liabilities like rent payments," Mayur adds, elucidating on the struggles of the first few months. However, if you ask the optimistic duo about what pulled them through, "goodwill and positive energy", they reveal with a smile. Also, to their merit was the goodwill and positivity they share with their father who helped them to pay the rent for the first few months when the business was slow.

"While depravity was always a pinch to the ego, it was also a constant reminder and motivator for us to do better and to make the best of the faith that our parents have shown in us," Swapnil speaks with a heart-warming insight. In the world of entrepreneurs, where competition and aggression rules the moods and relationships between people, it is indeed relieving to see this familial bond and principled positivity that also reflects in the bond of the brothers and what makes them so affiliated and affectionate towards each other.

It has perhaps been this unending belief and support the brothers have offered each other through the thick and thin of the development of their enterprise that has helped them pick many feathers in their cap in the three years they have been functioning. With over a hundred and fifty clients, the enterprise has now built its name as one of the most efficient service providers that are known for their out of the box technology solutions and for the perfection in the servicing, both qualities that give them an obvious edge in the fast expanding industry. It is not an exaggeration to say that clients that have received products in this unique enterprise have always left happy and satisfied for the value of money. This is also one of the biggest reasons that has helped them build a consistent and loyal base of customers who try to avail a plethora of services from them. People would earlier take them lightly because of the apparent belief that skills of a person are necessarily equivalent to the age. Because of this, the young entrepreneurs had to try hard to prove their worth amidst a horde of clientele that looked upon them as inexperienced young blood. However, it was the valor of this young blood that kept them at their persuasive best and inspired them to impress customers with their work. Although lacking in marketing or business experience, the brothers stayed adamant about building a strong brand value reflected by the way they treated their customers and the kind of services they provided. Indeed, this endeavour paid off in the end, as small assignments started leading to big projects, customer persuasion converted to service seeking calls from the client and most importantly, how incessant follow-up calls for petty payments evolved into advance payments from the clients – all became proof of the faith they had built amongst the target audience.

"This required a lot of development from our end too. Not only did we have to stay motivated, no matter how bad things were, but also enhance our own understanding of marketing and business management skills because we had negligible knowledge in this and that could possibly have led to our downfall," Mayur shares candidly.

It was also this inherent drive to keep moving forward, productively and creatively that got the brothers to think beyond convention, routine and the acceptable business pattern that a stable three-year operation schedule had got them into. It was with this aim to look beyond the horizon and to make the best of the gift of their skills and knowledge that a new initiative kindled into their enterprise that gave them a definitive platform of innovation and inspiration. In the month of August in 2014, after the enterprise had relatively stabilized and a relatively consistent source of work and revenue had been established, a phenomenon polluting the Indian environment for the past many years came to Mayur's attention.

"I happened to read in an article one day that about one lakh children go missing from schools or other educational institutes and are deployed into the darkness of human trafficking, beggary or simply for ransom," said Mayur, "I couldn't sit peacefully after that for a while. I don't have children of my own, but I do know how vulnerable they can be; their distress in a situation like that would be devastating!"

Anyone who knows the brothers personally would vouch that the siblings are the kind of people who believe in actions a lot more than words. This attitude is probably the reason why after learning about this situation and researching further about the cases around the country, they decided to do something about it and put their skills to use in a manner that could potentially work as a solution for this grave issue. Thus came their initiative '360Track' which was aimed to help parents, guardians or teachers to keep a track of the whereabouts of the little ones. After deliberation and experimentation, the duo came up with a model of a card-based system wherein the elders would be intimated when a child left the premises of the school, tuition or hobby classes. In consultation with educational institutions and parents during their research, they built the model connected with Student Management System which will offer security as well as automation. Keeping in mind the necessity for diligence, accuracy and ease of access that was needed for such a system, 360 Track was designed with an automated communication device that would send messages to concerned sources without manual intervention. This also included features like access to academics related data for parents; one-to-one chat system for institutes, teachers, parents and students. With the aim to make the service accessible to a maximum audience, the software was designed on all interfaces as a mobile application and most importantly, made extremely affordable so that monetary limitations do not come in between a parent and their child's safety.

Such endeavours have not only helped Swapnil and Mayur in succeeding professionally in multiple dimensions of their interest and passion but also helped them grow closer and stronger as brothers.

"Working on the child-safety application was an insightful experience. We are both unmarried but are very close to our family. This bond, coupled with all the research we did with schools and parents helped us to analyze the depth of a child's psyche. These discussions often took us back to our childhood as kids and how we looked out for each other. We envisioned 360 Track to be like a protective brother, to look out for the kids out there!" Swapnil explains warmly. They say you never really know the best of a person until you have seen the worst of a person. Swapnil and Mayur may have grown up together, fought and played together, but it has certainly been this journey with Horizon Technologies that has shown them the worst and best of days with each other.

"There are good times and bad, agreements and differences, successes and failures. But the key is to stick together and always look out at the bright side of things; that's what we do!" says Mayur.

Between the two, with their individual skills, experiences and interests, the brothers also split their roles within the enterprise. Having now grown from two people to a team of more than twenty committed members, they have given the organization a shape of effortless and collaborative mechanism. While individuals are encouraged to come up with dynamic ideas and to excel in their respective roles, it is an unsaid bond of respect and acceptance that helps the brothers, along with the other team members to bring different opinions to the table for discussion.

"We always encourage differences, sometimes even clashes. This is because it encourages a healthy environment of listening and accepting – something that will help individuals go a long way as a team," Swapnil – now the Business Head of the venture says. Mayur, on the other hand, handles the technical aspect of the enterprise and also functions as the CEO of Horizon Technologies.

It is through a conglomeration of events, struggles, lessons and decisions that the brothers have come to the stage where they are now. From clients won through several rounds of interviews to convincing their credibility with small steps of achievements, from having their father help them out with the rent to rising to a point where they can afford their own pool of talented employees, Swapnil and Mayur have risen strongly in a span of three years. One maybe amazed at how certain decisions help to shape what lies ahead of us. The brothers began with their own enterprise as the beginning of their career, without joining any other job or seeking experience in the so called conventional stalwarts of technology in the country. Some may call this a big risk while some might have even said that they were being foolish to risk everything. But today, just like the very first day the brothers made their decision to start their enterprise, they stand confident about their decision. Even with job offers at hand, they had gone ahead with their instinct and faith in one another and today, that very bond between the brothers has brought them so far out to the horizon of success.

 To know more about 360Track and how it has revolutionized the communication between parents and educational institutions, visit www.360track.in or follow them on Facebook: /360Track.

Zainali *(left) and* **Azra** *(right) started up* **Good Stuff** *to uplift artisans by roping them under the head* **Alpha Cube** *to customize clothes, shoes and other things of everyday use.*

Strokes of Dreams

Alpha Cube by *Zainali & Azra*

"This won't work", they said, "not even for a day. You need something constructive, something that has a future. This art and craft is a good hobby but at some point of time you need to get serious." They had stamped their words, the verdict had been passed and obviously there was no space for negotiation. 'They' are a decisive entity in the lives of most of the people, especially in a country like ours. They condition minds into a certain kind of education and profession, among other major founding decisions of life. They are not always wrong, but unfortunately, they are not always right either. The 'they' in question here are a bunch of well-meaning people – family and perhaps friends of family, who had sat together to decide the fate of one Zainali J. when the decision was made that the apple of their eye would become an engineer because, well, there was a future in it, and because that's what a million other people in the country seemed to be doing. Well, obviously there had to be something right about that!

Thus began an excruciating journey of a long haired boy, a misfit amidst aspiring engineers in the city of Mumbai.

"My entire childhood had been spent doodling, sketching and drawing on every scratch of surface I could lay my hands on," Zainali confesses, "And there I was stuck with something I couldn't bring my heart to enjoy."

11

It took many bored lectures crammed between two years of his engineering classes and a million curses that he hurled at himself before the vagabond finally broke out of this compulsion and dropped out of college. And if you are beginning to think that this was the point where his life magically turned into a movie script where he became a hero, this is not one of those stories. It was here that a series of experiments, trials and errors began for the young man who was struggling to find his feet in a world that so far has only been drawn between the lines of convention, stability and rationality. After having rejected one of the biggest hallmarks of a stable career in India a.k.a being an engineer, Zainali tried his head, hand and heart at different work experiences like working at a call center, being a disc jockey and even modeling, among other seemingly 'unreal' choices of profession, according to his parents. He was never the kind of boy who is idealized in a family. He always had his mind in his own world, going with the flow, breaking conventions and driven by an aggression to achieve. "Although a people's person who would crack people up with his sense of humor, my brother was always considered the black sheep of the family," speaks his younger sister, Azra, with a tone of non-judgmental understanding.

"This one is a nomad – that's the right word for him, he can't stay in a space for too long neither can he stay without scribbling, drawing something for too long," Zainali responds teasingly to his sister's comment. In that first interaction between the two you can tell that this relationship roots way deeper than the seemingly average sibling rivalry. Having understood and accepted that the brother-sister duo would have to beckon a journey that would break conventions and lead them into a partnership beyond their personal relationship, one that taps on their avocation and interest along with bringing them to a direction that would shape their career path.

When the hearts and minds of these two crazy and creative souls combined, an expression was created. Alpha Cube began its journey with innovative, custom made hand painted shoes. There's quality and aesthetics and then there is the uniqueness of every design that distinguishes it from any other piece in the world – that's what Alpha Cube is all about.

"It's really a reflection of us, you know! Individual, powerful souls, we have formed our own shape, molded our own individual colours, like the shoes, each of us fitting into an individual life," Azra speaks with philosophical insight.

Alpha Cube was one of the very few equations Zainali had managed to solve and the word stuck around in his head. "I like problem solving, you know. And this particular problem had a ring to it, so I guess it stuck in my head and surfaced when our creative venture started formalizing," Zainali recalls.

So what got them stumbling from engineering and art to creative designing of shoe art? Just the instinct that pokes each one of us deep inside our hearts when we see something that happens to be our calling!

"Doesn't matter if you like cooking or painting or designing or constructing; you have that one moment when you see someone's work and think in your head that you can do way better than that," Azra expresses candidly. "Most of us ignore that instinct and move on with whatever we have been conditioned into doing. We didn't."

Her recollection will take you back to the fateful day in a flea market in Juhu when the siblings came across a stall that held a pair of hand painted shoes, among other things. That was the moment of "we can do way better than this" for the brother-sister duo. Except that they didn't walk away into the fluff of their worlds forgetting about what they can or cannot do.

"Before the next market day, we had a pair painted and ready. Having convinced a friend who runs a stall there to display our hand painted shoes and hand out our business cards, we took the first step of acting towards our dream," says Zainali.

Again, this isn't a Bollywood movie, so there wasn't a queue lined up to buy that one pair of 'fish eats fish' artwork on a pair of shoes. There weren't many enquiries but a few people took the business cards that the friend had to offer. And then there were endless moments of anticipation, with the duo expecting calls from prospective buyers or seekers. It took a lot of patience and three days of waiting before they got their first call and consequently, their first order and as Zainali explains jubilantly, that's how they rolled into business!

"But it wasn't that call or that order or that first designed shoe or even that flea market that turned us into entrepreneurs," he adds clarifying his disposition, "this happened long ago in our heads when the decision was made to step away from the clutter of concords, when I had decided to move out of the family business or when Azra had picked up her degree in fine arts; our journey had started long ago when we had heard our own instincts and more importantly, resolved that we would do only that which we love, no matter what."

While for Zainali, to satisfy his parents with an acceptable degree they wanted still took priority, Azra had an easier time convincing them to let her pursue higher studies in fine arts, simply because unknowingly, her brother had already fought most of the battles for her.

"My folks had seen the consequences of pushing my brother into conventional education, they knew better than to try that stint with me," Azra jokes although with no intention of hiding her relief. While Zainali had been given his undertaking of exploration before joining the family warehouse business, Azra too was sanctioned a year where she was allowed to explore her own interest of profession. That the brother-sister pair coincided their interests and passion into a business opportunity was not only a stroke of luck but a much needed break that they needed to explore their creative expression and to break away from the pressure of conventional paths. The end of 2008 marked not only the appearance of a path that the duo could pursue professionally, but also officially brought them into business in the form of Alpha Cube.

However, to say that it has been a smooth ride since would be a bit of a romanticized hope. "There were times we had tough decisions to make, work to juggle with, responsibilities to complete and of course, my own education to finish," Azra explains looking back at the ups and downs of Alpha Cube. "And obviously these were times I counted on my big brother to help me with the right decisions and to keep on with this pursuit, no matter what."

The equation of sincerity and accountability that the siblings share with each other is impeccable and can be labeled as the major reasons why the two have gotten through this very unconventional choice of profession.

"There have been times when we have been receiving orders for merchandise for corporates which would mean a slight digression from Alpha Cube's intended core. These are the times when I have made the call of giving our venture a slow pace so that Azra can concentrate on finishing her education and the enterprise can concentrate on building a strong hold and recognition," Zainali explains. Name and recognition came to the duo with their hard work and uniqueness quite early in the journey of their enterprise. Having been featured for their cool quotient and innovation in entrepreneurship on two of the most popular shows on national television, and having found coverage in national and vernacular print media, Zainali and Azra have carved their own niche in places where it matters. They have already found respect that translates into loyal and persistent work assignments by some of the most prestigious names of the country. This only goes on to validate the ethos of pursuing one's true calling that makes events, almost mysteriously, align in favor.

Speaking of how favors have turned the fate of this brother-sister pair, a series of events can be traced back into churning them into a name with big accomplishments. Not only did the engineer-artist duo win contests at national levels for their extraordinary shoe art, but also got a platform for visibility and recognition that led them to being introduced to several companies for whom they eventually became their long term merchandising partners.

"I was hesitant in the beginning, because I honestly had no experience in apparel designing before these endless requests and offers started pouring in," Zainali speaks candidly, "but I knew I wanted to give it a shot and I knew I would come out having learned something better than worse." This attitude of optimism, coupled by Azra's endless support brought the young explorer to evaluate the market of apparel designing – from stitching to printing, and this brought him to the experience of the skilled workers in the slums of Dharavi. Though they started from Dharavi, they moved to Chembur a year-and-a-half later, after gaining some experience and knowledge to cater to brands and move out of the corporate manufacturing space. Their workshops are currently in Chembur.

"I knew I had found the right set of people to work with, and honestly, it was possible to go ahead and get work done even with the given situation, but I couldn't turn a blind eye to their situation," Zainali reflects with a look of determination on his well-meaning face. Thus began a more structured journey from a carpeted floor and a couple of machines and a gem of a tailor master to an almost empire like set-up with two factories, over eighty skilled artisans and tailors and over a hundred machines. They have diversified with specialized segments for the men's and women's sections and diversified from shoe art to apparel painting, designing, and mural painting for cafes and prominent structures and even graphic designing.

For those who have felt that the impossible is a dream, these siblings turned co-founders have set an example that breaks all conventional beliefs and rules. Even though challenges have come in different forms and voices for the duo, they have managed to convert even the worst times into lessons that have only strengthened their trust and equation with one another, along with the respect and trust they have earned from their clients, as well as their family.

"We still sometimes laugh thinking about the innumerable times our family had expressed their fears and opposition towards our pursuit of this passion," Azra giggles only knowing better now, "Especially about how Zainali had been labelled the black sheep when he decided to drop out of college. But we have come a long way from there."

But you see a pair of well experienced eyes scanning the entire production floor, ordering things around while scrutinizing the figures in a heavy register and you know the siblings have managed to win both the trust and the support of the family as this pair of eyes, that belong to their father, watch over them with pride and confidence as he himself has joined Alpha Cube on their request to support financial and administrative challenges that only experience can tackle.

"Having him onboard has been one of the best decisions for us; not only does he help to look after the operations effortlessly so we can focus on designing and clients but simply having him around is a big boost to our morale," Azra speaks with a fondness of familial affection.

Affection and solidarity has found its way into the lives of Zainali and Azra and everybody around them in more than one way. As firm believers in karma and the power of energy that can change the way the world revolves around you, the duo have tried their best to convert their expression of art into something more than merely a commercial transaction.

"One of the biggest reasons behind setting up the factory for the workers in Dharavi was to provide them with humane and hygienic working conditions like clean drinking water and toilets," Zainali explains. The purpose of art, according to the duo, is to uplift and create a sense of harmony, "and that would be a fake objective if the people who are helping us realize this dream are not themselves happy and harmony," adds Azra insightfully.

In the process of building more production units, not only have the young entrepreneurs been providing skill training and employment to a lot of people from the lowest strata of the population in Mumbai, but they have also been supporting their staff members in socio-economic aspects of their holistic development. Whether it is the education of children of the employees, liability of medical treatment or even support for an employee's daughter's marriage, Alpha Cube is oriented towards the welfare of its family. It is then, not for reasons unknown that the staff support to the enterprise has been unconditionally committed.

"We are all like a family here, celebrating each achievement together, looking out for each other and standing up for one another in the times of crisis, no matter what."

For the believers, this would go on to explain how a young pack of two seemingly naïve artisans have travelled this adventurous and long journey from battling for their choice of education to running their own manufacturing factories with recognition and work coming from all over the industry, ranging from corporates and designers to Bollywood celebrities and top media channels.

"Manufacturing for domestic and international brands taught us a lot. Although we were painting and creating art, manufacturing had indeed become our core business. We knew we had to infuse art and creation in this aspect as well," beams Zainali.

"Armed with a mission to uplift the artisans, we work with art as our weapon of choice. We launched our clothing brand Good Stuff, where art meets fashion!" Azra backs up enthusiastically.

"Why Good Stuff?" Azra smiles and elaborates, "We believe in art as a form of upliftment. We create positive experiences. Do Good, Be Good, Feel Good."

Legends have it that professional and personal climbs have varied footsteps. To say that relations at work affect relations in personal lives would not be a far stretch from reality in most cases. But spending one day with the siblings will reveal a contrary truth. Not only is the duo exceptionally compatible with each other in terms of their skills, management and coordination, but it is also a delight to fit in like a puzzle, complimenting each other, enhancing their strengths and correcting their weaknesses. This pair teams up together against the world, or more suitably, to embrace the world. This is not to say that differences in opinion don't arise; but with the harmonious equation in their heads and hearts, Zainali and Azra are clearly headed in the same direction, only for the better. With absolute respect of space, individuality and decisions, the spine of their equation lies in the unconditional confidence and trust that they share with each other.

Sharing every little achievement as a proud moment, every feat as a step forward towards their endeavour and facing every challenge as an experience that is meant to make them stronger, Zainali and Azra have brought about a world of their own, one that has broken conventions and digressed to create new definitions of success and pride. They have undoubtedly changed the meaning of entrepreneurship along with proving to the world that no interest and no direction are small or wrong when the instinct of the heart is followed. Alpha Cube and the story of the dedicated duo is certainly an example to look up to, to rediscover long lost dreams and to fulfil them with the right people, at the right time.

You can check out some fun merchandise on www. goodstuffofficial.com. Follow them on Facebook: /goodstuffofficial or /AlphaCubeCustoms.

AppVirality *is the brainchild of* **Ram** *(right) and* **Laxman** *(left), helping apps acquire, engage and retain customers effectively.*

Siblings Who Work Together, Grow Together

App Virality by Ram & Laxman

The legend in the Indian mythology entails that Ram ruled a large kingdom in the country, many centuries ago. He was accompanied by his younger brother Laxman and together, they undertook many journeys, fought many battles and defeated many enemies of their empire. Among the many stories that come out of the tale of the two brothers, the most common factor was that irrespective of their individuality and perspectives, the brothers stuck with each other, no matter what. When the elder brother was sent on an exile, Laxman followed him, surrendering his own life, to be with his brother. Similarly, Ram looked out for the well-being of his brother, no matter what came their way. The combined force and dedication of the two brothers helped them make many friends, associations with different kingdoms, join hands with a strong and loyal support system and ultimately run their empire peacefully. Of course, there were a few other agents of goodwill and support that helped to achieve all of this but even today, after thousands of years since the story originated, the brothers have been immortalised for their dedication towards each other, their loyalty and unconditional support, so much so, that examples are

21

made out of the Ram-Laxman pair. Even in modern India, parents fondly name their children Ram and Laxman with hopes that their bond will be as strong and legendary as the mythology. To see such an example in real life is both reassuring as well inspiring.

One such example of brotherly bond with the namesakes is that of this modern pair of Ram and Laxman who have carved their own niche in the field of innovative enterprise. As brothers, they have grown up together with similar interests and experiences and received the same values and principles in a simple, traditional Indian family. While Ram pursued his master's degree in Electronics, Laxman chose Computer Applications as his subject for post-graduation. Having studied in the same university, the brothers also received a similar ambience once out of their home to pursue higher education. However, this seemingly conventional duo has broken the codes of a safe and stable path and set out on their independent journey to create their own story.

Having pursued his education in around the subject of computer applications, Laxman then diversified into the path less chosen of a career in social media. He began blogging out of sheer interest, which grew into a passion and eventually organized into a pursuit. It was not long before he had managed to create a network of 3600 bloggers from different backgrounds, working together on content development. Thus, a large hub of creative minds was created to provide content for different mediums of advertisement for a plethora of advertising agencies. Despite having kicked off well in this direction, Laxman has never been the kind of person to stay complacent in any one direction of growth. Soon, his endeavours found him starting an online grocery store which, in many ways, was the predecessor of the likes of BigBasket in today's online marketing diocese in the country. This young entrepreneur established and ran this venture efficiently for eight months and then came to the point where he realised that this was a capital affair – something he did not envisage himself pursuing as a long term plan. But the young entrepreneurial mind was bent on building something out of ordinary and the passion for this pursuit convinced him to tread away from the conventional road and build an enterprise.

Ram, on the other hand has been drowned with the passion of tech running through his veins. Fiddling with the latest trends in the world of application development, the tech-guru has been making innovative inventions for many years now. His applications have not only been used by several to fulfil the most basic necessities of daily lives but also been appreciated and rated amongst the top of their league. However, satiation at the slightest mark of success does not run strong for either of the two brothers. Ram, with his eagerness to know and develop his applications better came across challenges that he personally took upon to solve and eventually, even convert into a business idea. One of his most acclaimed applications is based around live user information for routes, schedules and running status of Hyderabad local trains. Needless to say, that while for the users, this turned out to be a blessing to make their lives a lot easier, for Ram, this was a revelation of an opportunity.

"I realised that there wasn't an existing growth hack that could help to track the progress and help an application grow organically. This is when it struck me that I needed to address the base issue before and beyond anything else in the world of application enterprise," Ram explains the circumstances for the genesis for what later became the full fledged venture that the brothers started.

With the idea of starting a growth hacking toolkit that could help applications and therefore start-ups and enterpreneurs,

Ram approached the only person he relied on undoubtedly for professional or personal support – his brother Laxman. And thus began the stride of the brothers to build a game changer in the world of applications, made famous by the name of AppVirality.

Having begun as path breakers, the innovative entrepreneurs have already acquired more than two hundred applications as their clients who are now successfully using the growth hacking tool to their advantage. After having first acquired some of the stalwarts of startups in the Indian market as its trusting customers, AppVirality has expanded to a rightfully earned international customer base across nations in Europe, Asia and America. Within a few years of their launch, the brothers have already managed to accomplish a loyal user base and results that have won them acceptance and acclamation as pioneers of growth hackers. Like the attitude and ambition of their enterprise, the choice of the name of their venture also reflects their direct, focussed and transparent policies.

"We wanted a name that would hit the nerve, just like our product. Applications have been looking for effective growth supplements for a while now, and here we are to address the core of this issue,"explains Ram knowingly.

However, the accomplishment that the duo has reached in the last two years since their launch in 2014 have been layered with a plethora of challenges, some predictable and some as surprises out of the corners.

"One of the most obvious challenges was to get our family onboard with the idea of product that they did not even understand," Laxman speaks in retrospection.

Like a scenario in a conventional Indian family, the idea that the brothers would both quit their jobs and venture into something unpredictable was a little tough for their family's acceptance and took a while to achieve. However, to say that this reaction was a reflection of the apprehension that the siblings had struggled through themselves too, would not be far from reality.

"I have to admit it was the toughest decision to make," Laxman confesses candidly. "To leave a stable job is not easy. Although I know that Ram's idea was masterly and that the application had the spine to crack what it would have taken to make it, we were both new to the world of entrepreneurship and there was a lot we had yet to learn!"

These learnings came in different forms and timings, a lot which, the brothers define as trial and error. To put together a team, which currently stands at a strong strength of eleven members, has not been an easy feat either. This came with trial and error, stringent filtering and extensive searching for the best fits.

"It is one thing to work with your brother as a partner but a completely different league to find like minded people and bring them together as a team. That can make or break a deal," explains Ram.

With challenges of funding dangling for the initial phase came the stake of maintaining a balanced act between quality and expenditure. "This is where things got tricky for us and I wish we would have had a better idea of setting targets in advance for everyone. It helps to have the road maps chalked out; that's been the biggest learning in this venture," he explains insightfully. However, with the right attitude and approach, the siblings have managed to overcome both the operational as well as strategic challenges with an open mind.

"Our experience of working with some of the best brands of the country helps. The approach is to get to the most effective solution with best results. We try to prioritise and keep away from distractions," Ram simplifies the challenges as opportunities and attributes a lot of the enterprise's success to the hurdles that has helped them grow stronger every moment.

It is not only their professional focus and experience that has gotten Ram and Laxman ahead in this game-changing spot. The two brothers are undoubtedly the brain and spine of the enterprise with each other's support and that's what makes this business-like equation a long way beyond board-room discussions or client meetings.

"Ever since AppVirality clicked in my head, it has been Laxman that I have turned to for setting the building blocks of the venture with me. He compliments in the areas where we need to work together and understands exactly what I need," Ram speaks fondly of his brother. Everyone who has worked with partners in enterprises or even at regular jobs can vouch for the risks involved. This includes reliability, compatibility and even basic competitiveness that are all factors that have potential of making the equation vulnerable. However, your sibling is someone you have grown up with, lived through thick and thin of life and who inadvertently means well for you.

"It is a big relief to know that the person you can connect with and blindly trust in your personal life is also there to watch your back in your professional life. That really helps to concentrate on bigger things and take leaps with the faith that you have their support. What makes this equation even more fitting is the complementary nature that gets the siblings going along; where one lacks, the other excels.

"As siblings, we know the strengths and weaknesses of each other, we know what ticks or clicks with the other person and therefore, it makes it a lot easier to stand up or back down at appropriate moments – whether it comes to decisions, deadlines or even meetings with the clients," Laxman explains the partnership mechanism, "keeping honest communication with each other has helped us make this quite effortless through the years, even before

AppVirality, when we had worked on other projects with each other."

With this compatibility quotient comes an ease of distribution of work and key decision making diocese.

"Ram is an excellent coder but doesn't handle sales discussions on a day-to-day basis very well. So he handles the tech part while I handle operations. It is an effective equation."

However, to say that their roles are mutually exclusive would not be appropriate. The brothers maintain an equilibrium of independence and symbiosis all at the same time. While decision making in key areas of expertise is both trusted and respected, both Ram and Laxman are often found to share moments of updation and consultation with each other.

"Responsibility is not the tasks assigned by profiles, it is more like taking ownership of the bigger picture and doing what's best, without considering boundaries or egos," Ram reflects insightfully, clearly signifying the equation that the brothers have evolved in their work space.

When it comes to work and family, most people draw a line somewhere. For most, these two aspects of life exist as separate entities and mean differently with different priorities. However, the enterprising siblings have given a new meaning to the definitions of personal and professional spheres.

"Our understanding of 'work' is not something to do with making money or building an organization. It is passion that pursues us to live and build and progress. It doesn't matter whether we are at home or in the office, AppVirality is a choice of life that makes us want to make everything better," Ram shares passionately.

The brothers have been investing into their personal equation just as much as their professional endeavour. It is no surprise then that their relationship with natural affection has also been accepted and encouraged by their respective spouses too.

"Both of our spouses have been the backstage heroes in this venture. To accept what maybe our sometimes overwhelming involvement in work and to encourage us in the risks that we take speaks volumes of the strength of these women who I can proudly claim to be the backend support behind our success!"Laxman reveals candidly.

Battles between siblings have known to lead to the fall of empires, break families or lead to catastrophies that last for lifetimes. Sometimes, the siblings won't look each other in the eye and rage war at the slightest of triggers – these are all facts that we have witnessed plenty of times around the world irrespective of backgrounds, culture or discipline of equation. However, to watch Ram and Laxman excel in their bond – both professionally and personally, is not only praiseworthy but inspirational. But is that only an assumption as an outsider?

"You would only be telling half the truth if you thought we don't battle!" Laxman jokingly exclaims, "we battle with our brains, bring differences to the table and sometimes question each other's decisions for days. But that's one of the best parts of our equation. This helps us bring different perspectives and passion to discuss for the enterprise because we both want the best for each other and for AppVirality and I don't see how it could be any better than discussing and deliberating on the key decisions with each other."

With trade and technology, patience and passion, the siblings have managed to overpower a diversity of odds. Starting from an idea that was an existing challenge to the world of applications, their expertise has managed to turn the hurdle around into an opportunity of invention. And this, as some of the most accomplished people in the world would say, is the essence of the mettle that successful people are made of. Within two years of designing and launching their enterprise, Ram and Laxman have succeeding in not only bringing measurable success to their credit but also managed to build a reputation that has spread through the user experiences that their clients have witnessed. More than anything else though, it is the equation that the brothers have metamorphosed with each other, both as individuals and as brothers, that makes them really proud of each other. With values of trust and understanding, not only have they created an enterprise for growth hacking but also perhaps hacked the key to their personal growth as well!

 To make your apps grow and go viral. Visit www.appvirality.com and follow them on Facebook: /appvirality and Twitter: @AppVirality.

Himanshu *(left) and* **Varun** *(right) started off with* **Aspiring Minds** *with a vision to inspire, assess and acquire talent for educational institutes and organizations.*

Inspiring Aspirations

Aspiring Minds by Varun & Himanshu

When Plato said that beauty lies in the eyes of the beholder, it is possible that he meant it in more ways than one. While appreciation of all things good comes to someone who holds an elevating perspective, it can equally be said that he who seeks, finds. For someone who is looking for trouble, it may not be difficult to bump their legs or fate at every corner of life. While if someone is seeking opportunities, solutions or offerings, they will seek the best ways to make this work too. This philosophy makes the foundation of dividing the world into two kinds of people. There are those who work for their centered goals, achieve and satiate their focus in that position of achievement. Their comfort is both their cushion as well as their veil. The other kind of people, however, are the ones who have focused, achieved and yet, refuse to be gelled down in that complacency. They are the kind of people who are not centered on their own accomplishments alone, but strive to provide the same around them. This may involve stepping out of their comfort zones, breaking down and rebuilding their notions and sometimes, even risking personal losses. And yet, these are the kind of people who earn a lot more than money can weigh. Such are the kind of people who make it bigger accomplishments than personal victories, and clearly, such are the people who are remembered in stories to be told for a long time to come.

One such story of people stepping out of their comfort zone is that of the brothers Himanshu and Varun. With sharpness and intelligence in their DNA, it comes as no surprise that the brothers made their names into the most premier institutes of the country and also the world. However, where most accomplished people draw the line and continue their paths in reaching milestones after milestones of personal achievements, the siblings decided to grab this definition of success and give it a twist that would change the trends of how other people find access to success.

It is no secret that a creamy layer of the top performers in every field of vocation and academics get their choicest direction of pursuit, whether it be desirable brands to work with, effective profiles or discipline of academic achievements. But what happens to the rest in queue is a backstage story that doesn't even reach the appreciative mention list. What adds to this anomaly is the fact that while job seekers across the globe can't seem to find the right job, a horde of organizations can't seem to find the right people suited for their needs. It is almost like a giant jigsaw puzzle of jobs is floating around in the globe which more often than not, seems to be failing to find its perfect fit. For those who have found theirs the story ends right there. So should it have ended for Varun and Himanshu, especially keeping in mind the level of their achievements. However, made of a different mettle, the brothers have been wired to think differently, and beyond the personal spheres of needs. It is perhaps this way of thinking that brought them to a point of deliberation and innovation that helped to bring many scattered pieces of a puzzle together for thousands of people.

"It all started a few years ago when I was still in pursuit of my master's degree in MIT. I stumbled upon a research report presented by Mckinsey that burst my bubble of comfort about job security. I found out that the employability situation of the common Indian engineer was in a bad shape," Varun recollects that the statistics which disturbed him claimed that only one in four engineers in India are employable at the current state. This triggered a disturbance in his heart that led him to change the course of his career to do something about the situation of employability in the country.

Before finding out what happened next, it might help to get an insight into what goes into the making of the siblings. While it is commonly believed that one has to be of an extraordinary stature to accomplish extraordinary milestones, both Varun and Himanshu have proved that it is more of extraordinary will and strong actions that can make a stalwart out of seemingly mainstream personalities. Hailing from a family that has churned necessity into creativity and built ideas for education, the brothers have received education in the form of traditions and experiences – a luxury that life does not afford to many. With a vocational degree in Computer Science from an institute known worldwide for excellence, Himanshu also has earned experience of working with international organizations in the US for five years. This was his time of learning and displaying skills of accurate and actionable results, all meeting the high standards of excellence that boasts of international demeanor. Varun, on the other hand, with his extensively research oriented brain has been more academically instigated. Having written his first successful computer program while studying in the fourth standard of school, Varun finds deep fascination in genetic algorithm which got him oriented into pursuing his Master's degree as well as a PhD in the subject at MIT. While making steady academic progress, Varun was also inclined towards philanthropic activities. CURE – Coalition to

Uproot Ragging in Education – an initiative started by Varun back in 2001, for instance, was founded with the intention of preventing the abusive practice of the ragging of students of various ages. It is evident that both the brothers were doing well of themselves by impressive standards. And yet, it was their extraordinary thinking that got them to change the course of this perfectly stable sail. The reason behind this exceptional turn is also understandable at a closer look into their lives.

It is said that the apple never falls far from the tree, the case of Varun and Himanshu proves that in both their substance as well as motivation, that comes from an academically inspiring father who has been a pioneer in initiating computer education in schools and also a well-known in the world of academic books. The brothers also draw their entrepreneurial skills from him. This comes as both an advantage and a relief. Anyone belonging to a simple middle class family in India would know the challenges of having to break away from conventions, especially if it involves venturing into the world of business of unconventional products or services.

With such an acumen and environment, it is then not very surprising that the brothers chose the path they took as professionals, entrepreneurs and philanthropists. That one moment of the state of professionals in their country had been trigger enough to send the brothers into an explorative journey of how they could help the situation. This is when the analyst and the researcher, the thinker and the programmer, Himanshu and Varun came together stoically to find a solution.

"We realized that while everyone had been creating different kinds of education and training programs to fix employability, the need for scientifically defining employability was important. Our idea was that if the same could be assessed using automated assessments and made available to all students in the country, not only would it become a fair and scalable mechanism for corporate to access talent but would also provide detailed employability feedback to our young prospective workforce."

This ideation was followed by a series of deliberation, research and some of the best scientific methods in the discipline were brought into the picture and combined with the innovative approach of the siblings. And thus, with the efforts of the dynamic duo, an oath breaking entity was born in 2007 with the name as enlightening as its purpose – 'Aspiring Minds'.

In their own words, the entrepreneurs describe Aspiring Minds as a global job skills credentialing leader which was set up "with a vision to create a merit driven talent ecosystem and enable efficient job skills matching by crafting credible and intelligent assessments," Himanshu explains. The enterprise is basically a platform for individuals to analyze their own skill sets to understand their capacity and appropriateness for the most fitting jobs. It also provides them with recognized credentials and directs them through the right channels towards jobs that will complement their profile. On the flipside, Aspiring Minds completes the entire loop by also providing recommendations to organizations across the globe on the basis of the most fitting candidates for their desired profiles, thus making it a win-win situation for everybody in the loop. With the help and support of the positive eco-system that the brothers have built for themselves, they have been marching forward in this journey of almost a decade now and made it strong not only for themselves but also for a number of people.

But with incessant accomplishment comes responsibility and humility that shows its presence in simple statements that the brothers make in casual conversation. When you congratulate them for bringing this unique idea into such a strong and successful shape of reality, they shrug it off with a shy smile. "We have been inspired and supported by so many people who deserve credit for this," they say. Their mentor, who they express immense gratitude is Tarun Khanna, professor at Harvard Business School, helped them with the foundation of this enterprise through his guidance and wisdom. One also hears deep respect in their voice for their father's contribution in their life.

"I think the will to do good and to do it in the best way possible, has come down to us as a lifetime of learning handed down in the family. We owe a lot to our father for that," Varun shares candidly.

Along with the academic streak, the siblings also take after their father for the entrepreneurial zeal they exhibit in running their venture. Thus, a lot of what they have accomplished comes as no surprise to the family that has worked hard to raise the boys in a manner that makes them grounded and ambitious all at once. Painting a strong picture of what family does to the integrity and achievements of a person, Himanshu also extends his gratitude to his wife who has been a constant pillar of support through his battles during the initial phase of the venture through all its uncertainties and risks.

"It helps to know that someone is standing strong as a supporting pillar, no matter what. I think she has shown more confidence in me than perhaps even I have held and that helps me stay consistently strong through the ups and downs of this entrepreneurial journey," he adds humbly.

It is no doubt that such an environment, that the brothers have created around themselves, has only helped them lunge forward with consistent learning and evolution.

However, like any battle for evolution, the struggle of Himanshu and Varun has also shown them several shades of blues. Despite their personal experiences with academic research, organizational functionality and technological understanding, it took a while for the siblings to find their footing in the world of enterprise. "There was a lot we still had to learn," Varun reflects. "It was only once we rolled out the plan did we realize that several nuances need to be addressed a lot differently when it comes to building your own enterprise."

At the genesis, Aspiring Minds was funded by the brothers from their own savings. While the idea behind their model was perfect both in quality as well as appropriateness of application, it can't be denied that entering into a new venture, which did not have a precedence to draw inspiration from, could have been nerve bending to say the least. Despite their educational and professional credibility, to get such an unconventional idea to settle with their potential clients was also a task they had to address with a lot of deliberation.

"Back in the days of 2007, start-ups were not in vogue like they are today and were seen as more of a risk than a strong move in career growth. You can imagine what a nightmare this would prove when it comes to hiring a strong, dedicated and capable team!" Himanshu exclaims.

However, if the brothers had been the sort of people who would have been intimidated by kick-start challenges, they wouldn't have left the luxuries of their own trajectories of professional excellence anyway! On the contrary, the siblings worked hard to build a platform that would not only personify excellence of product but also become a name people would aspire to attach themselves with. With this determination and a consistent endeavour of a decade, Aspiring Minds now stands strong with about five hundred employees dedicated to the organization. With a brand value that has both credibility and impressive return on investment, the venture has risen from baby steps to mammoth leaps of associations with about 3500 companies, organizations or entities that now value Aspiring Minds for their head-hunting requirements.

This evolutionary journey has also taught the brothers the art of cooperation and understanding that has helped them sustain and improve through this journey despite mutual differences. "As siblings, it is natural for us to be as different as chalk and cheese," Varun explains, "but during the course of building Aspiring Minds, it has been our privilege to get to know each other more intently and holistically."

With their individual sets of skills, experiences and motivation, both Varun and Himanshu bring forth a plethora of opinions, decisions and suggestions to the table. It is then very obvious that often only one of them gets to have their say. In ordinary sibling equations, this could lead to massive distancing and ego-clashes. However, for this pair, these differences have been welcomed with an open mind as the brothers have learned to respect each other's opinion, as well as to coordinate with each other for the larger good of their enterprise.

"Another thing that has helped us in this partnership is the fact that both for the sake of convenience as well as efficiency, we have divided diocese amongst us in a manner most suitable to our acumen and expertise. Not only does this help us keep our reach more decentralized and diverse, but also gives enough space to us as individuals for key decision making in our respective areas of responsibility," Himanshu explains.

It is perhaps this equation of trust, understanding and mutual respect that has brought the brothers to this stage where they have become the founders of a venture that is one of the most widely used platforms for skill analysis and job recruitments around the globe. With rising popularity and strength, the siblings have also worked diligently on their responsibility, efficiency and innovation to always stay ahead of the game.

"There is a lot of competition out there, through conventional as well as unconventional mediums. But the idea is to always be on the edge, never to be complacent with the current status and to always analyze what it would take to help us grow bigger and better," Varun speaks insightfully.

With such an insight that boasts of both knowledge and experience, a partner who is more than a co-founder and a supporting eco-system comprising of well-meaning family, friends and associates, and promoters who believe strongly in Aspiring Minds, the venture stands as a true symbol of the genesis of its name.

"Both of us are deeply touched by Late Dr Kalam and find deep roots of our motivation in his book, *Inspiring Minds*. This is what inspired the name of our brain child and continues to inspire the ethos of well-being, excellence and synergy around us," Varun reflects with wisdom. This has been a partnership worth drawing inspiration from both in personal as well as professional dimensions. Both for inspiration as well as aspirations, the collaboration of the siblings is resonating in many levels of excellence in the entire cycle of professional ambience of the world.

For more information on automated assessments to pump in some more self-confidence, visit www.aspiringminds.com, Twitter @AspiringMindsAM and Facebook: /myamcat.

Blueprint *is the brainchild of* **Navya** *(left) and* **Divya** *(right), aiming to celebrate the individual and their state of mind, translating self-esteem into personal style with bold silhouettes.*

Blueprints of Sisterhood

Blueprint by Navya & Divya

They say that the true test for bonds are the distances of time and space put between them. If you want to tell the difference between a real and fake bond, you watch it over time. If it withers away, it was never the sort to fall back on. However, if it builds despite the passage of time, you need to hold on to it with dear life. Similarly, distances add to the test of bonds as litmus adds to acid or base. Whoever coined the phrase 'out of sight, out of mind', had obviously witnessed the heartbreaking end of the deal. On occasions where geographical or even social distances have only made people realize each other's importance in their respective lives, you know you have earned yourself a gem of bond – for a lifetime! Now, what you make of this bond then, or which other fires of strength do you put it through is entirely up to you or to your fate. Sometimes, fate lets us take our chances in such cases, and sometimes it has already taken the chances on our behalf and landed us with the relations to sit along with all our lives, waiting to be doubted or sprouted.

Navya and Divya are like two banks of a river, two doors of a car or two sides of a coin. In elucidating the relevance, they have lived together, grown up together and stood by each other since childhood. More as friends than sisters by birth, the duo have experienced life through thick and thin. They received an environment and encouragement that nudged them towards exploring different disciplines of life, even as children. The sisters were often found doodling, sketching or painting moments from their dreams or realities back in their childhood. With an environment that promoted them to explore their creative instincts the girls grew up with a plethora of experiences and a confidence that allowed for them to fearlessly discover areas that interested them. As adults, the duo diversified further in their educational, professional as well as personal experiences. From communication to art, from teaching to corporate profiles, Navya and Divya have walked paths through diverse verticals, adding to their skills. They credit a range of learning that has helped them build their future endeavours. Even during the pursuit of their individual life choices, they have managed to stay connected and in sync with each other's lives, despite being geographically distanced. While Divya had pursued her career in India working for fashion designers and gaining experience in the domain, Navya, after spending a few years in the country in pursuit of her career, had moved to the US after getting married. She continued to learn and experience new territories in foreign land while focusing her attention towards different art forms – a passion that has been her focus since childhood.

While in their own individual spaces, these creative spirits were still exploring possibilities that would allow for them to experiment with more challenging and enterprising opportunities. This journey took a concrete turn when one fine day, Divya called her sister with a proposal that changed their life henceforth.

"I was actually at a friend's place. But when Divya called, I could tell from her tone that this would be something extraordinary," Navya recalls about the genesis of their entrepreneurial journey together. It was during this time that the younger sibling had pitched the idea that two sisters start their own apparel brand and work together as business partners.

"This idea of starting something of my own had been bugging me for a while. I guess the thought was just waiting for the right moment to mushroom into actualization," Navya explains. It was when she felt she had acquired the appropriate experience and insight into the fashion domain that she felt appropriate to dive in with her own reign.

"What better way than to begin this with someone who has been my partner in crime through life?"

The sisters have always looked towards each other for matters of support, solace and solidarity. For big decisions or small chit-chat, they are the first names that cross each other's minds. More than companionship, it has also been a matter of compatibility in interests and ideas that inspired Divya to turn to her sister with the offer of co-founding her dream into a project of reality. With a mix of talent and trust, creativity and collaboration and passion and patience, the dynamic sisters finally launched their fashion label 'Blueprint' in the year 2011.

If a reader believes that compatibility and companionship alone can get two people to work their magic on any venture, this is an illusion of a novice. Very clearly evident through the struggles of the people who work through the many barriers to make an adventure lucrative, stories of successful enterprises come with long tales of mishaps and mistakes waiting to be corrected. Divya and Navya have also battled through their own share of hurdles ranging from creative clashes to managerial road blocks. It has only been this roller coaster which they have ridden that has brought to them their most basic and critical lesson.

"To begin with, our biggest challenge was to function in sync through different time zones. For us to be able to coordinate and collaborate in two different continents, to be available for brainstorming, firefighting and rolling out of sales, we needed to be available together, actively. Obviously the time zones did not work in our favor!" Navya jokes in retrospection.

As much as the sisters battled through this challenge and adjusted their entire lives around the mission of making Blueprint work, there were also uncontrolled external factors that needed micro-management. While the sisters were progressing to build their collection of women-wear, they were also dealing with background struggles of finding the right kind of suppliers, artisans and platforms that would help to realize their 'blueprints' of ideas.

"We had gone all in with our savings. This was a major source of motivation as well as intimidation for us," Navya shares candidly, "We knew this was our chance and that we had to give everything to make Blueprint work."

The fashion industry is a busy one, there's innovation happening with every passing moment in the world. With penetrating technology, it is convenient to be known and heard anywhere across the globe if you have the right skills. While this fact is an incentive for the domain, it also underlies a major challenge in terms of space and risk of over-exposure.

"There are many players in this sector, both local as well as distantly originated. So the competition is fierce. If you are anything in the league of the ordinary, you're sure to be lost," Divya speaks in complete seriousness about her understanding of the situation. It is in the battle of beating the competition that the sisters have attained most of their learning from. Starting from scratch, they worked upwards on everything that an enterprise comprises of. "You would think that to come up with a creative range of clothing that breaks the clutter would be the toughest part, but for us, that actually was a lot easier than handling the functional challenges of Blueprint," Navya reflects.

For two people passionate about design, Blueprint meant more like an expression of their ideas. But the logistics of back end coordination and marketing effectively is what put the siblings to task.

"Even once your collection is ready for sale, there's so much more to do in terms of pitching it in the right manner, catering to a clientele or simply being able to retain the channels that have been established in the market; it needs a lot of focus and hard work." Clearly, the sisters have shown no dearth of that ever since the day of the launch of the enterprise, which has not just become an important part of their lives but primary their life itself.

Having dedicated their lives to the enterprise, the sisters have come this far not without the support of their family and well-wishers looking out for them. The designer entrepreneurs claim themselves to be lucky because their parents been extremely encouraging and supportive towards their decision to plunge into their own venture, which, as per conventional standards, is a high-risk break-away from the trend that most Indian parents approve. Navya, who lives with her husband in the US has also found unconditional support and guidance from him in times of need.

"It is true that for a successful woman to climb heights in her career, she needs the understanding and support of her family, especially her life partner. I am lucky to have found that."

With the ecosystem conducive for both the sisters, they are able to focus on the more important issues. Between video calls to match different time zones and follow up actions in their respective arenas, the duo has also labored to build a clientele that is not only loyal but also works as prominent brand ambassadors in the limelight of the fashion industry. Although the initial collection launched by Blueprint was appreciated by the audience, it took them an extensive marketing strategy, campaign and collaboration with fashion bloggers to make their presence felt in the right bracket of customers.

"Every collection that we come up with takes months of deliberation, arguments, research and rejection before the final product is approved. But it is what you do with the collection, how you pitch it and endorse it that makes it successful," Navya explains with experience.

For the duo too, the real shaping up of success and walk into the limelight happened when they had personalities like Sonam Kapoor and Richa Chaddha, to name a few, bequeathing their outfits. This big leap of publicity became a boost for their sales and later, proved to be only the beginning of what became a rally of endorsements from celebrities across industries. This benchmark was followed by their appearance in the Lakme Fashion Week – a feat that positioned them amidst the exclusive few amidst the fashionistas of the country.

This seemingly ironed status of Blueprint has its history of crucible with the sisters battling through time zones, rejections of ideas and designs and innumerable conversations back and forth along with discussions with the *karigars* (artisans). With the accomplished pedestal that Blueprint has earned, one would think that a web of thinkers and implementers would be involved in this foreplay of art.

"We're actually just six people at the core of Blueprint!" exclaims Divya taking you by surprise. "Navya, myself, our two tailors, and two girls in the finishing department, who do the ground work from end to end."

One of the reasons of keeping this a close-knit affair is to ensure quality control.

"We want people who are in sync with our ideology, who understand the ethos of Blueprint and who are tuned into our style. We are lucky to have found the two artisans to fulfill these requirements."

However, step one for the two sisters has been being able to sync with one another. If you were to imagine the chaos that siblings as kids indulge in with each other, the nature of their conflicts and differences, you would be right to believe that a lot of this does not change even as adults.

"I would be lying if I say we don't bring conflicts back home with each other. Sometimes, to agree on the design, on the collection or even the look-book there is a lot of clashes between us which takes a lot of communication back and forth to resolve," Navya reveals in earnest. However, it is the trust and understanding that the two share that has brought them to a stage where they respect these differences and welcome them to the table for healthy discussions.

"I am glad we have different opinions. This helps to broaden the horizon and choose what is best for the enterprise," Divya exalts. It is also this clarity in their understanding that has helped them evolve their roles and responsibilities as partners. While discussions and brain-storming happens through video calls or emails between the sisters irrespective of their timelines, Divya and Navya have eased into a mechanism of seamless flow of work from charting of ideas to actual pitching of the final product. While Navya helps to work on designs, Divya coordinates with the fabric suppliers and artisans. As the former decorates the final presentations and look-books, the latter formulates Blueprint's presence amidst the fashionistas and media channels. Although there are no assumed positions and boundaries between the duo, they are well aware and respectful of each other's strengths and interests and have always strived to bring the best out of each other and themselves for the venture.

Apart from the fact that Blueprint has been consistently doing well with its collections ever since its launch in 2011, in terms of both quality as well as visibility, the success of this entrepreneurial accomplishment is also marked by the personal growth that the creative sisters have experienced since the genesis.

"There's no doubt that this was the best decision of our lives, and I can speak confidently for the both of us in this," Navya smiles with the warmth of a loving sister. From that fateful phone call that the sisters had, there have been challenges, lessons learnt, failures and achievements – a roller coaster ride that they are extremely proud of. But more than anything else, it is what this enterprise has done to their relationship that the sisters can't stop relishing.

"It is like we have gotten to know each other in a new light altogether. Having been through the best and the worst, with stakes involved on terms that are very dear to us, we have learned to surrender to trust and respect for each other. The rest has been history!" Divya elates with an honest expression.

While Blueprint has been making its own founding mark in the world of fashion wear, Divya and Navya have been setting their own example, intentionally or not, for many aspiring women to learn and follow. It is a partnership that has broken conventions, overcome challenges and carved a promising path for the women and dreamers across diversities to take that step which is keeping them away from their reality of accomplishments. The siblings have been an epitome of excellence in both personal and professional spheres. While their professional equation teaches how diversity is an advantage that helps to fill the missing pieces of a puzzle, it is also a reinstatement of the fact that partnerships do not stand ground on the basis of two people thinking the same thing but two people thinking in favor of the same thing. It is the differences in opinions, or different opinions brought to table in earnestness that leads to the holistic success of any venture. This professional ambition is also a reflection of personal symposium that the duo share as siblings turned friends. Not only has their understanding of each other's strengths and weaknesses altered with this experience but also helped them to understand the depths of their compatibility with one another. It is their complete faith and respect for each other than has metamorphosed with the passage of every challenge, failure and success that they have witnessed together. This learning has undoubtedly been the blueprint of the growth of their success and certainly continues to pave the way for many more milestones that the duo is due to achieve in the years to come.

To try out apparel that's a perfect blend of elegance, colour and print, visit www.designbyblueprint.com or follow them on Facebook: /Blueprint. by.Navya.Divya.Niranjan.

Sidhhartha's *(left) skill with his patented technique* **DPOL** *and* **Shreya's** *(right) strength to back him up led to the establishment of fashion wear brands August and Aight, and their flagship store Pret Castle.*

Enterprising Beyond Bonds

DPOL (Direct Panel on Loom)
by Siddhartha & Shreya

Imagine a story of Hansel alone in the dark forest fending his way against the crafty witch without Gretel to stand by him in his fear. Imagine if Jack had gone to fetch that pail of water alone and had to deal with the big fall and the tumbling all by himself without Jill following! Even the legendary Scout from the pages of the best literature in the world would be incomplete without the role of good old Jem in his life. The best of history has been established by the most awesome siblings who have not only accompanied each other through fun and frolic but tumbled along with each other through adventures and risks. Not only do they make an awesome pair for creating havoc through the most organized social set-ups, but also back up as the most efficient partners in both personal and professional dealings of life. Whether these are little adults who look out for each other and cook mischief to the best of their abilities or coordinate as matured individuals in matters of trust, siblings are known to make the best combination of emotions and practicality. It is no surprise then, to see that even in the world of enterprise across the globe, many siblings are weaving innovative start-ups with innovative equations.

51

Like all siblings that have created history, defied norms and turned the tables around to establish their bonds beyond the ordinary, Siddhartha and Shreya also have a legacy in motion that makes for a story worthy of inspiration. Educated with a pedigree to be proud of, the brother-sister duo hail from a background that enriches their knowledge and experience in field design, marketing and information technology with bachelor's and master's degrees. It was Siddhartha's passion towards innovation in technology and his will to bring it to good use for the world. During the second year of his graduation in Engineering, the young lad invented a revolutionary technology for green fabric which he called Direct Panel on Loom (DPOL). It was this design that led him into an intense discussion with his elder sister, Shreya when they met after a period of two years. Shreya had just returned from one of her tech-based projects in Australia and was very curious to know about her brother's latest developments.

"You couldn't help but be moved by his passion. Not only was his invention a product with path breaking potential, but Siddhartha's business idea and conviction was also very thought provoking," admits a clearly impressed Shreya.

What happened next was a commitment of investment, between the brother and sister.

"It was a promise that included but was not limited to financial exchange," Siddhartha recollects, "It was more of an investment of goodwill, faith, patience and belief in one another that brought us to the beginning of our enterprise." While Shreya brought home a plethora of experience in some of the most renowned organizations of the world, with her stature and exposure to working environment in India, Australia and New Zealand, Siddhartha had to his credit a recognition of his patented product that precedes its reputation. DPOL has been acknowledged as one among the top nine sustainable fashion innovations across the globe to change the future of fashion by Discovery Channel and the UK government and has earned a place in London Science museum. Currently DPOL has over 3000 international publications globally in fashion magazines, fashion research journals, academic textbooks and is a topic of study, research and dissertation in leading fashion colleges round the globe.

DPOL was also invited at COFES (Congress on the future of engineering software) a Silicon Valley conference in the USA which is organized by CYON research in collaboration with NASA, Lockheed Martin, Xerox etc.

This connection in a professional dimension proved to be a combination that made them an instant hit. Shreya and Siddhartha launched their product – fashion wear brands – August and Aight that are retailed from their flagship store Pret Castle in Greater Noida and designer stores in India and worldwide.

"I have grown up with her, we have learned, played, laughed and cried together… it was only natural that we would go on to explore the world this world of enterprise, clubbing our skills and strengths together," Siddhartha explains.

You can tell that the duo seems very comfortable with this professional equation with their constant and organic expansion in their enterprise and with new ventures that they keep undertaking with higher milestones. In 2015, the siblings released their co-authored book called *My Fantastic Failures* – their telling of the rise and fall in life and how it helped them make the best of their situation, with each other by their side. Furthermore, the duo has also ventured into the food business and opened their first café that runs by the name of Serendipity. With each achievement, the partners in dime and destiny have carved their niche only strengthening their confidence in the 'investment' they have continued making in each other for all these years.

August and Aight, with their unique positioning as patented sustainable fabric that is world renowned, have made their existence known and acknowledged on Indian as well as international platforms. As symbols of grandiose, confidence and the attire for a vibrant and smart generation, both August and Aight pride themselves as brands of western wear that provide clutter breaking style and fabric technology that is purchased by loyal clients all over the globe.

"We are a part of the national and international fashion fraternity. We have exhibited in the Lakme Fashion week in India, Ethical Paris Fashion week in France," Shreya speaks with a well-earned tone of pride.

It has taken a lot of selective designing, sincere hard work and motivation for the duo to let their brands come to a position where it speaks for the values and principles that they had intended for them to stand for.

"The idea is to provide women with fashionwear that is comfortable, with good quality and affordability and yet with a quotient of fashion that makes them unique in their own special way. It is our deliberate intention to steer clear from projecting women in stereotypical appearances," Shreya shares an insight on the perspective of the clothing line that has fast been gaining popularity with its panache.

Humanists, animal lovers, plant enthusiasts, out of the box designers and visionaries these are some of the adjectives that can begin to define this duo that has come a long and laborious way to make their joint venture a success. While Shreya is currently dedicated to expanding their fashion clothing business and systemizing the food business located from Auckland, New

Zealand, Siddhartha continues to live in India and handles the enterprise as the director at August Fashions and Pret Castle. With a combination of creativity, science and business, Shreya attaches business aspect to Sid's creative products.

"There is a fine line between creativity, art and business," says Siddhartha, "Shreya efficiently helps to bridge the aspects."

In turn Shreya says, "Sid is immensely talented and hardworking, it is he who does everything but gives credit to me."

The mutual respect and importance they hold for each other in their life is the reason that they have come so far. It is not by sheer luck that the siblings have become entrepreneurs, neither is it a chance that the duo chose to work with each other.

"Our parents had always encouraged us to pursue our entrepreneurial streak, to take risks and build our own path rather than follow the safe road. This was probably one of the biggest cushions for us to know that we had their support and confidence. This meant a lot when it came to quitting a safe job and plunging into this venture," Shreya explains with an undertone of gratitude that the two feel for the family. This can be accounted for a lot of brave decisions that the siblings have managed to make, whether it was about defining the uniqueness of their clothing brand, scaling international platforms or even diversifying into food business.

"Mom and dad had treated us as matured and responsible individuals even when we were kids. We have been brought up in a way to be respectable towards our resources and to take risks when it comes to exploring new avenues in life," Siddhartha recollects with pride. It is then no surprise that the duo have found complete confidence and reliance in each other, sharing the same principles, conviction and passion for their entrepreneurial acumen. Behind this accomplished duo, is the spine of parents, spouse and well-wishers who have had their own share towards this achievement. Shreya's husband, Sapan, has been a symbol of support, inspiration, guidance and critique in times of need for the siblings. While the family has exalted in this venture from the very beginning, the achievements of Shreya and Siddharhta owe their credit to organizational, creative and entrepreneurial excellence – assets that the duo has acquired while growing up.

"I remember our father used to leave us little notes whenever we came home. These would be some inspiring quotes, excerpts from works of literature or something he felt would be meaningful for us. In his own way, he has been teaching us to read, explore and find our own meanings in experiences that life presents us with," says a deeply contemplative Shreya.

The key mantra that drives the life of the brother-sister also helps them make the right decisions for turns that decide both their work and life.

To say that the journey for Shreya and Siddhartha through their ventures has been a smooth ride full of achievements alone would be a half-truth at best. The challenges, fears and failures that the two have had to experience, accept and eventually overcome have been plentiful too.

"To raise the initial funds, we travelled across the country looking for the right people to invest in our idea. But that didn't work," Shreya continues to explain how the challenge was not in finding the people to bring money for the venture, but the problem was to find people who wouldn't want them to compromise on the principles with which the siblings wanted to set their enterprise. This was when she decided to invest in her brother's idea and for them to begin the venture together. It was this initial lack of funds that held them back from quite a few significant aspirations, which they believe, in retrospection, would have helped them push their fashion line on a bigger and more lucrative platform.

"However prepared you'd like to believe you are to face the risks of an enterprise, you can't turn a blind eye towards the stakes involved. Your job, your relation with the partners, the finances and even the norms or the people you have pushed to choose this path – these factors loom in the background that keep you on the edge," Siddhartha reveals with candid honesty.

However, these challenges have served as lighthouses for this duo to tread their path with caution, patience and utter respectfulness to the available resources at hand. "Notwithstanding the fact that we have we been constantly pushed to make do with the limited resources we had, but this has in-turn encouraged our creativity, strengthened our business sense and walled us against the risks since we couldn't afford to make many mistakes."

Siddhartha has come a long way with these learnings from a patent in the second year to being a globally recognized brand. First, his selection in the Lakme Fashion Week in 2010 won him national acclaim and then, with being featured in the fashion week in Paris put them straight out on the global line of vision. This was subsequently followed by the co-founders buying a store and starting their path on retail themselves in 2013. Not only did these events bring them the opportunity of a massive business boost and visibility in markets at both national and international level but also worked amazingly to encourage them on their endeavour.

The experience of working together, has however, not only helped them grow exponentially in their business and skill sets, but also helped tremendously in the deepening of their bond with each other.

"We have travelled, built, brainstormed, haggled, innovated, won, lost, laughed and stressed together; all of this with the experience of becoming entrepreneurial partners beyond being siblings," Shreya speaks laughing at the thought of all the fond memories. She reveals that differences have arisen on more than one occasion between her and Siddhartha pertaining to decisions in the business. "But at the core, we are the same – we come from the same roots, believe in the same fundamental values and envision the same future for the enterprise. And hence, our agreement is headed for the best."

Having divided their roles categorically, the siblings adhere to the major decision making and implementations in their own department. While Siddhartha heads the creative front of the fashion wear brand, Shreya handles the business end of the deal. Although, it would be unfair to say that a few solicited steps into each other's domain are not uncommon. While the duo believes in maintaining their individual streaks, it is also equally true that they respect each other's opinions and advice from the heart and often welcome perspectives and inputs from each other to enhance their own horizon.

"Even if we are having a fight as siblings, on personal issues, if one needs the other at the work front, the other is unconditionally present for support and suggestions, keeping aside any qualms," speaks Siddhartha rejoicing in the reliance the siblings share with each other.

Whether they handle mutually exclusive ends of the business, or work on the same project, whether they live in different continents or hold meetings under the same roof, whether they work on different domains or burn the midnight oil to win the same clients, this dynamic duo has a bond that outshines any boundaries of personal or professional equations. They thrive beyond the limitations of ego, credit, domination or position. Like little games played together in childhood, encouraged and inspired by their parents, Shreya and Siddhartha have grown up to only strengthen the equation of commitment and selfless well-being for each other. Despite having their own different circles on the social and perhaps even professional fronts, the two are deeply connected in the vision and principles of their enterprise. While many find it hard to even look in the eye of their siblings after a certain stage in life, the brother-sister pair does not even need to look into each other's eyes to know how they feel. Having extended this warmth and well-being with Shreya's husband and their parents, they radiate a sense of protective and yet carefree aura created around the family. While most do not believe in tales from books that are centuries old, Shreya and Siddhartha sure take you back to fantastic stories of brother-sister pairs that have found their names become famous in the pages of history.

DPOL	DPOL as a smart technology saves lead time, water, effort, and even money. You can know more about fabrics inspired from it at (need web links).

Prince *(left) and* **Rohit** *(right) started off* **Eleve Media** *to enable marketers to explore and use efficiently effective advertising strategies based on content.*

Explore, Engage and Expand

Eleve Media by Prince & Rohit

Scene at a dining table, somewhere in a house in New Delhi. Little Ryan skips from one lap to another, his mischief enlivens the mood of the gathering where three adults are sitting together and are engaged in what looks like quality time with family. An elderly couple is seen relaxed on the couch, watching television and reading the morning newspaper. Two gym bags can be seen in a corner, there are clearly some members of this family that work out. Cups of tea are doing the rounds on the table and something is being discussed with great animation by Prince. Rohit, a visible contrast in demeanor, is level headed and nodding calmly at the excited expressions of his brother. Kritika, Prince's wife, is juggling between her son Ryan's constant demands of dropping objects off the table and the interesting conversation that is going on between the brothers. They duo keep turning to her to ask for her opinion and she duly complies. For an outsider, this may appear as a Monday morning discussion amongst family members. Perhaps they are discussing the next holiday destination? One may wonder.

One couldn't possibly be more wrong. What appears to be 'quality time with family' is actually a diligent business discussion going on between the trio. This is exactly how they spend their mornings before diving head on into their daily activities. These activities vary from conducting hands on meetings with the team to reaching out to new clients for business development; from responding to emails to personally attending customer briefings and looking after a toddler to seeking guidance from senior advisors. This is, after all, what Prince and Rohit – the brothers responsible for revolutionising web marking perception – envisaged. Eventually, Prince's better half chose to come on board too, while keeping in mind her own personal responsibilities and engagements for the family.

Hailing from the surging town of Bareilly, with its hems skirting around the hustle and bustle of Delhi, the siblings have nurtured ambitions in their hearts from breaking away from the ordinary and pushing their limits of passion.

"We are both inclined towards finding a rush in life. It is success we chase, no matter where we find it," Prince explains with passion. The duo, apart from sharing the same blood line, also share an enthusiastic interest for blood rising hobbies like super biking, paragliding and travelling to adventurous places in search of everything that life has to offer.

"We have found an immense bond that brings us closer with experience, with every loop at the bike race tracks, every new destination explored or simply, every new personal record set at the gym," Rohit shares with a gleaming smile. It is perhaps the routine of these material engagements that the brothers share together that bring them together at an emotional level as well.

"Our experiences in our lives have taken us on individual journeys. With different attitudes and choices, we have been able to earn a variety of skills and interests," Prince speaks reflecting on their education, and first few years of professional experiences.

"However, even if a tree has grown many different branches, it does not sprout different roots and shares the same primal characteristics," he continues suggesting the equation that the siblings share despite their many differences. "We may be different in our approaches, different in words and even in our silences," Rohit adds poignantly, "but we have been each other's support system since either of us remembers; I am sure Prince echoes my sentiment." He receives a warm nod from his younger brother. After witnessing this warm and amiable equation between the two, one is bound to wonder what has led them to be what they are today, both as brothers as well as business partners.

"It is difficult to mark any one particular day and say that we kicked off our idea from that moment. But everything did start taking formal shape a few years ago when Prince walked into the house and declared that he had quit his job," explains Rohit. If it had been any other Indian family, a huge conundrum would have broken loose. However, this family has its very unique and logical way of approaching life and that is what works as their strength at the core.

"Ryan was only about four months old when Prince broke this news to us. We had all discussed this in the past... but watching it in action was a different story altogether!" Kritika exclaimed with excitement at the memory. Although there were financial responsibilities to uphold, Prince had thought this through in his head and deliberated the idea of starting something of his own, before putting his papers down, taking a break from the routine job that was bowing him down and beginning the action phase of his dream project.

"It is, after all, in our blood to build something of our own," Rohit explains. "Our father ran his own successful business in the pharmaceutical industry till sometime back. It is only fair that we carry forth his legacy. Prince had to take the first step and we followed suit to build the enterprise."

Having worked in the digital space for around five years, the brothers had learned the tricks of the trade and understood how the system works inside out.

"It was during this time when we were both working with reputed organizations in the country that something came as a realization worth converting into a business opportunity." Prince throws some light on the huge market gap in the digital world for brand perception and amplification.

"See, the idea exists in isolated clouds and has been worked on in a random fashion. Our idea was to bring this into an organized and highly efficient channel with the help of technology." With this determination in mind, the brothers founded Eleve, their brain child in June 2013, although it had conceptually been formed quite a while ago in the hearts and minds of the family.

"Eleve as an adjective in French stands as a universal word for anything on top of the order. In our case, we think of it as 'advanced'. Our vision is to be the pioneering and leading advocacy solutions company in India and be synonymous with innovation and user experience," Prince elaborates. Just like any other instance, Rohit complements the idea further by adding his two pence to the table, further breaking down Eleve's role as an influence marketing platform that enables brands to create and amplify brand perception on web and social web. In the simple words of the co-founders, it's a human network that creates word of mouth through well written posts on blogs, Twitter, Facebook, Instagram and Youtube. This human network consists of bloggers, influencers and celebrities. The technology behind gives a post campaign analysis that helps brand evaluate the success of the campaign.

One would think that content projection is not a new phenomenon in the market. However, a clearer understanding of how Eleve functions and what its unique selling points are can be made with further probing questions to the siblings.

"Advocacy has existed in this arena, however we were the first ones to organise this by our proprietary technology that was based on six key objectives – Scale, Automation, Measurability, Accountability, Transparency and Feasibility," Rohit expands on the tech features further to show how the tool will cater to owned advocacy needs through their own employee influencers. It is with these core points of uniqueness that the brothers have brought Eleve, with its tagline 'Creating Talkable Brands' to its pinnacle of success today with clients from across the country and growth rate that shot over 250% within a couple of years of operation and has brought them to a position where Eleve is taking its first few steps this year into international waters.

However, the enterprise that has begun to move leaps and bounds on its climb to success did not always have glory served on a silver platter.

"It is hard to believe now that the initial days of Eleve were spent in a garage, next to a casino!" Kritika recalls. With judicious expenditure as a priority, the idea of saving every penny was duly respected by the team. "When we began, I couldn't afford an office space. I had very little savings and we were functioning as a bootstrapped start-up," Prince elucidates about the beginning of Eleve. "It was here that I convinced Kritika to come on board and step into my shoes while I went ahead to bring business. Obviously, she was apprehensive because she did not have the expertise of this vertical at that time. However, the positive dynamite that she is, Kritika, as usual, proved to be an unconditional pillar of support," Prince reflects affectionately.

With her as a reliable team member, Prince was better able to concentrate on making sales pitches and building contacts for business development.

"I still continued with my mainstream job for the time being," Rohit narrates, "so that we can keep the financial pressure at bay. I was contributing simultaneously to Eleve and the three of us would sit every morning and evening over numerous cups of tea to build our strategies, collaborate developments and brainstorm on all possible directions for growth."

Gradually, the trio was able to generate and deliver enough services for business that they could afford their own office.

"That garage, oh man!" Prince exclaims with child-like excitement. "It was one of the most elevating and humbling experiences at the same time. I remember there were times when we would be very tense over a serious discussion or be in a fix, trying to resolve some problem and suddenly, a huge cheer from the casino next door would declare someone's flamboyant victory. That was all it took to make us burst into laughter and ease the tension!"

It was with such optimism and determination that team Eleve focused on its goal. "We always worked on the basic mantras, kept our expenses low, continuously worked on innovation and kept on delivering promises. It was these consistent guiding principles that brought us loyalty and well-wishes from our clients that eventually helped us stabilize," Rohit recalls the time when Eleve had managed to generate enough business so that he could afford to quit his job and join the team full time.

Behind these little steps of accomplishments, the brothers also witnessed a plethora of challenges. "I wouldn't call them challenges, you know," Prince refutes, "because it was these milestones that helped us learn our lessons and ensure that we have our feet set solid in the ground to prevent bigger damages." One of the most significant areas where they faced hardship was in bringing people on board.

"See to say things in a discussion is one thing, but when it comes to actions, people show their true colours. We had to learn this the hard way that people who we thought we could count on, could not really be there for us, whatever be their reasons."

To bring people to work for the team in itself is a major challenge. The siblings found it difficult to identify people who would stick to the cause and who could be trusted through the thick and thin of entrepreneurial road.

"However, we were very lucky to have mentors who came to us in the form of blessings," Rohit smiles with gratitude. "From guiding us in strategies, to helping us in recruiting people in the tech space (since neither of us have any idea about programming and felt clueless in making the right hire), we found seniors, ex-colleagues and even our parents, humbling us with their undying support and faith in us. The story of our journey would be incomplete without mentioning our endless gratitude to Mr Rajan Srinivasan, Mr Manish Vij, Mr Tathagat Sarkar and Mr Mukesh Marwah, who, in their own ways have held our hands, guided us, sometimes even helped us make difficult decisions and supported us psychologically, professionally and even financially."

It cannot be denied that the successful faces on large banners come with a team of people who work backstage in bringing their success to its actual form. Prince and Rohit have been undoubtedly blessed in finding such people in the world as well as at home.

"Bringing my brother and my wife on board Eleve was the best decision of my life," Prince speaks overwhelmed with emotions.

"After having stumbled through failures, counting on the wrong people, delays in financial transactions or even instances of people bad mouthing us out of spite, there is no word to express my relief when I come back to my two best friends – my brother and my wife, and their relentless support and optimism that I can count on with closed eyes."

It would be unreasonable to say that such proximity does not come with its cost. It is a widely known fact that professional partnership with family members is a classic recipe for disaster. One would wonder if this family too has seen the scars of such problems. Rohit smiles calmly and shakes his head.

"There hasn't been a time when I have ever felt that I would choose anyone else to work with. We have different opinions, we make different choices and yet, we organically, naturally and respectfully adapt into each other's systems; I cannot imagine being in this position, sharing this partnership with two better people than Prince and Kritika."

It is only believable then that the duo has split their roles with Prince holding the position of the CEO while Rohit enjoys being the COO of Eleve with mutual agreement and benefit.

Whether they are running on treadmills side by side at the gym or negotiating with a client for a project, the two have each other's back. It is not just the professional space that they share but it is also a road that takes them through their personal growth alongside. "There have been such profound moments of realisation, both in our successes as well as our failures, that we have seen each other and felt so much trust and affection. I can't be thankful enough to have my brother by my side," Rohit shares. Echoing the sentiments, Prince joins in with a kind smile, "I may be the elder one but Rohit has taught me plenty of things through this entrepreneurial journey."

Through ups and downs, through stressful meetings or team retreats, through evening tea time with Ryan and the parents and through crisis of faith and money in business, Prince and Rohit and been to the moon and back with their lessons and accomplishments. However, it is safe to say that the experience of breaking the norm, creating their enterprise together and battling it to victory through all its tides has been indeed brought them on top of the world – a true expression of Eleve for Prince and Rohit!

For effective advertising solutions and a gamut of options to explore, engage and expand, visit www.eleve.co.in, Facebook: /EleveMedia, Twitter: @EleveMedia.

An app-based fitness and lifestyle brand created by **Akshay** *(left) and* **Arushi** *(right),* **FITPASS** *is enabling users to choose to get fit where they want, when they want and however they want!*

A Fit-ting Partnership of Siblings

Fitpass by Akshay & Arushi

"It takes one to know one, I guess. That's what brings me closer to my ideas," he smiles and says. "And it takes two to make the knowledge work. That's what brings us closer," she adds with a wink. Sitting in their comfortable and inviting office, a space bustling with excitement and activities all around, the co-founders of this out of the box start-up look, behave and talk very differently from one another. But inside these seemingly different and somewhat opposite individuals are souls so alike that it makes them think and believe in the same principles, be on the same page, and ultimately the same goals. Akshay and Arushi are separated only by a few years in age and the choice of education they have acquired. But beyond that, they are joined by their entrepreneurial spirit, ethos of professionalism and above all, a kinship of blood. Meet the siblings who have been changing definitions of sibling-ship. Having grown up as partners in crime, the duo now stand strong as partners in dime and have started the entrepreneurial journey of their own start-up as co-founders.

In a country where individuals are pacing towards more adventurous tracks, to become a part of a start-up is not an unheard scenario anymore. People are seen to be leaving the comforts of well-known corporate houses, with established lines of services and defined roles and increasingly joining start-ups with innovative ideas and extra-ordinary work atmospheres. It still provides them the luxury of a stable income and yet helps to expand their professional horizon. However, Akshay and Arushi have left the guidelines of conventions far behind to set up their own model of enterprise, treading into a business domain that is first of its kind.

With an honors in Mathematics and master's degree in Financial Economics and Public Administration, Akshay has had the opportunity to study both in India and abroad. His perspective towards business is filled with ideas that challenge conventions and encourage him to look for business opportunities even in the most seemingly drab sections of the business world. Arushi, on the other hand, has pursued her bachelor's degree in Economics and a master's degree in Development Economics. Her exposure in national as well as international platforms of education as well as profession have instigated her to understand the purview of different markets and audiences, giving her an edge in the way she interacts with people and manages business relations. With these range of educational disciplines, experiences and skill sets, the duo brings to table diversities that not only add more value to the organization but also helps themselves broaden their own understanding and knowledge.

The leap from conventions came for the siblings around the time when Akshay finished his education and was looking at opportunities to explore to start his own venture.

"I was in no mood to join a full-time job and join the league of ordinary men," Akshay makes a point as a joke. It was this thirst to build something of his own that got him to watch and observe different scopes of business across domains. But as wise men often say, what you seek is never really far away from you. Both Arushi and Akshay, like many conscious and aware youth of today, are health conscious and believe that the key to a happy life is a healthy lifestyle. Since this area interests them, they try to keep themselves aware and updated about what is hot and what is not working in the health services sector. Keeping to the basic principles of a successful business, instead of building an idea and injecting it into the market, Akshay tried to identify a gap and work backwards to build a solution for it. He worked on the insight that lack of time and information often troubles health conscious people who tend out to miss out on their workout schedules because of these inflexibilities in most health services provided by their particular gyms or health centers. Encashing on this very opportunity, the young ideator built on the concept of creating an application to cater a more flexible and accessible network of fitness services to be made available to the target audience. The obvious next step was to find someone with whom he could convert this idea into reality. The answer to this quest came as both an instinctive as well as a logical response. He needed someone who he could trust, someone who could understand his ideas and someone who could complement his skills in building a revolutionary idea for fitness services. Basically, as Akshay clearly realized, he needed to partner up with his sister. Thus began the entrepreneurial journey of the siblings who have been rocking the world for fitness enthusiasts by providing a solution in the form of an application that grants what you seek. In 2015, they launched their dream child by the name of FITPASS - a disruptive app-based lifestyle and fitness brand that breaks all the barriers to fitness by making fitness accessible and affordable for the new-age Indian consumers.

"The beginning was filled with assessment, collaboration meetings, pitching, research and reactions all put together to form the spine of our application," recalls Akshay. "This was when we realized that it is one thing to ideate something and an entirely different ball game to bring it into an operational mode to actualize the dream."

One of the biggest challenges of being a path-breaker is the incubation period which the model takes before it is accepted in the market. FitPass also went through this phase when pitching to collaborating partners and potential users would hit the wall.

"People didn't understand the concept in the beginning, because there had been nothing like this before. While being unique can give you an edge, it can also take away the cushion of credibility that tried and tested products have," Arushi explains. And then there was the obvious technological inefficiency that came as a hurdle between the application and its users. "The Indian audience is still new to the idea of app-based services, especially when it comes to personal services. Despite having an accessible as well as affordable application, this was a big inhibition curtain we had to work hard to dissolve for our users."

Simplicity in the application as well as the model to make it legible was a way the siblings adopted to attract users. However, design wasn't the only thing the duo had to maintain their austerity in. Being a start-up that was bootstrapping all its expenses, the expenditures, especially in the beginning, also had to be kept modest. This surely deprived the pair from the aggressive and effective build up and marketing they would have ideally liked to start out with. However, Akshay and Arushi were never the kind of people to be pulled down in the face of challenges.

"We tried to turn around our challenge into an opportunity of judicious innovation and more importantly, rightful respect of all the resources we had brought together for the venture," says Akshay. Investing diligently in the right places and never compromising with the quality at any front is what the siblings worked hard for. This reflects strongly in the way Akshay and Arushi have put together their team for the enterprise.

"We both have had the opportunity of studying and working in the best environment whether it was with the top notch students in Oxford, or colleagues with extraordinary efficiency at the World Bank. If there's one thing we have learned from these years is that the most lucrative investment you can make is in the kind of people you choose to work with, and that is what we have done with FitPass," Arushi shares.

Having diligently and cautiously selected the people they interviewed and observed, the co-founders have sincerely built up the team. A proud family of twenty members now, FitPass offers excellence in its product, service and quality together, despite the operational and financial challenges it went through, simply rooted in the collaboration and cooperation of the siblings who dream and work together.

This climb through the struggle has had many levels of accomplishments for both Akshay as well as Arushi, a lot of them being intricately related to each other. From the point of the decision of partnership to the present date, these partners have been by each other's side, sometimes even at the cost of putting their individual stand aside.

"Even before I had completely formulated the idea behind FitPass, I knew I would be making that phone call to Arushi, asking her to join me in this endeavour," says Akshay. Counting his sister as one of his closest friends with whom he can fight and share at the same time, Akshay goes on to explain why she has been his first and only choice as a business partner.

"We have grown up together, and I know that just like during our childhood, she would stand by me, no matter what! Why would I even think about partnering up with somebody else when I have her around?"

It is true that as siblings, the understanding and trust that exists between any two individuals makes them confident about each other. However, in the case of Akshay and Arushi, even practical compatibility aligns them perfectly into the role of co-founders. Where one is a good ideator, the other is a good implementer. Where one can build, the other can bond and where one can calculate, the other can collaborate.

"If we were too alike in our direction of thinking and strengths of acumen, it would probably be easier for us to stay on the same page but not give us the kind of width and diversity we are able to offer to the business with our different interests, education and capacities. I think that is what makes this partnership an ideal one!" Arushi exclaims with a sense of delight.

However, this elated sense of belongingness in this business also comes after exercising a lot of deliberation and cooperation with one another. It is not like the dynamic duo has not had their share of differences.

"There were times, especially in the beginning, where we would have very contradictory opinions on important decisions to be made. These were some very challenging times for us and pushed our bond to its limit," she continues to share candidly.

However, with the maturity and insight that only people with a lot of wisdom and strength can exhibit, the siblings have learned over time to both accept and respect one another's opinions and decisions.

"We finally decided that we would keep our diocese in the enterprise independent of each other, and would only step in with suggestions or advice where invited," Akshay nods knowingly.

Not only has this decision helped them to make better decisions with a more focused and organized approach in their respective areas of leadership, but also helped them to draw the line in areas of conflict – an equation that the co-founders have sincerely worked on symbiotically. After deliberation and consensus, they have come to the final word that Akshay would handle the finances, technology, partners, customers and marketing, while Arushi would look after the partners and the customers. Not only does this bring smoothness to their operations but also gives the siblings an opportunity to focus on their respective areas of expertise and enhance their own skills to contribute to a holistic growth of FitPass. It is this balance and synergy that has helped them build a strong collaborative path towards the growth of their entrepreneurial efforts.

To say that this partnership is solely a professional feat for the duo would only be covering half the story though. In the process of building their idea, researching and reforming, overcoming the many hurdles and presiding over a giant ship as co-founders, the siblings have explored and experienced a side of their bond with each other that has brought them only closer together. "It is one thing to play and cry, share and dine with your sibling and to live together, yet leading your own individual lives, but an entirely different experience to partner up together in a professional and financial endeavour," Arushi shares.

Whether it is because the stakes involved alter considerably, or because the team effort starts affecting lives in a much bigger manner, not only of the siblings in question but also of many other people, such a partnership brings about a depth of equation that really makes an impact. "We have been pushing each other for better, supporting each other in moments of crisis, celebrating little milestones and consoling each other when things have been falling apart. I would earlier say that I believe in my sister, but now I can proudly say that I trust her with my life. Blindfolded!" Akshay declares with an affectionate smile.

Such is the bond and its growth that has brought them together as brother and sister. This amalgamation of personal and professional equation not only brings out the best in their venture, but also helps them tremendously to grow as individuals as well.

One might wonder what partnerships between family members do to their home equations. The situation between Akshay, Arushi and their parents seems to answer this in a pleasant and inspiring manner.

"We try our best to keep work and home separate from each other. We do this by following a strict 'no work at home' policy," Arushi shares. Blessed with a set of parents who have supported and encouraged them from the very genesis of the entrepreneurial actualization, the siblings share a healthy and balanced environment at home where parental friendship and sibling symphony reveals a content and progressive relationship. It is perhaps this level of contentment and support that the siblings have grown up with that has encouraged them to build such a strong bond, not only amidst themselves but also accounting for the reason behind creating such a respectful and cheerful environment amongst colleagues at the workplace of FitPass.

The ambitious siblings work hard and work sincerely towards the growth of their enterprise into a stronger and more widespread service. With over twenty-five thousand registrations achieved in only about eight months of operation, there is no doubt that this partnership will witness many more milestones in the times to come. It is heart-warming to see such positivity coming out of a bond between siblings in a world which is fast depleting of emotions and connections. Not only have they worked on a healthy and happy equation among themselves but also made a fit example for a good cause, a feat that inspires and enables people of the country to lead and live healthy and fit lives; that definitely makes them an enterprise worth learning from!

To choose your way of going fit, you can download the app or follow them on Facebook: /fitpasssocial, Twitter: @fitpassindia, Instagram: /fitpassindia.

Shravan *(right) and* **Sanjay** *(left) are two of the youngest mobile application programmers in the world, and* **GoDimensions** *brings forth their top apps compatible with Android, Windows and iOS..*

Age No Bar

GoDimensions by Shravan & Sanjay

When the opportunity to interview two young entrepreneurs who are making path breaking programs with a refreshing tone came my way, I was excited to meet the young minds. After all, the trend of enterprises in the country is favoring young minds who are fresh out with degrees or have a couple of years of industrial experience at the most. When setting out for the meeting, I was given their residential address, which is unlike most rendezvous points that start-up founders have. However, excited to get a closer look into their personal lives, I walked up to the comfortable looking house and rang the doorbell. Their achievements came flashing to me in this short period. That they have made some unique software applications in different domains, that they have delivered inspiring speeches in innumerable institutes and organizations of the country and outside and that their work has been acknowledged and appreciated by none other than our beloved ex-President, Late Dr A.P.J. Abdul Kalam, were a few snippets that rushed to my mind. From the various things I had read about them, I knew they were already striking the right chords in their sensitivity towards the utility of their products, holistic contributions they would make to society and the aid they would be able to provide to people in distress. Honestly, I was sold at that. But, unlike any other set of individuals I had ever met before, the biggest point of astonishment for me was that these programmers, brothers, co-founders and leaders were actually a couple of teenagers, still in school!

Shravan Kumaran is a sharp, witty and delightful boy of seventeen studying in his final year of school. Described as fun loving and amicable, Shravan has a diverse array of interests that includes playing the guitar, football and most importantly, coding that makes his heart race with excitement. Sanjay Kumaran, younger of the siblings, at sixteen years, is studying in the 10th grade. Like most other boys of his age, he too enjoys football, is crazy about his Xbox One and loves drawing Manga cartoons when he is not watching them on screen. However, unlike most kids his age, Sanjay is deeply philosophical in his thoughts and is a perfectionist in his perspective towards everything. Even more astonishing at his age is his keen interest in user design for products that he believes to be the key of any digital product.

It is this duo that has been driving the world of software application crazy with the sheer simplicity and brilliance of their work. The youngest entrepreneurs in the country and perhaps one of the youngest programmers in the world, Shravan and Sanjay have a strong motivation towards software development and towards addressing the most basic problems of everyday lives of people with simple yet effective solutions. It is this motivation, coupled with their extraordinary understanding and interest in the world of computers that got them hooked to coding. What began as a keen inquisitiveness towards the subject of computer science that was introduced to them in school, quickly evolved into deeper exploration on the subject. They further enhanced into training themselves in programming languages, graduated to animations and eventually mastered the skill of application development for different operating systems.

"We have both had a passion for coding, albeit different sides of it," Shravan explains, "and often we would come across situations which we thought could be solved with very basic application designs. Sanjay and I would often discuss what such applications would look like and how they will help solve a specific problem in the society."

However, there came a stage in the life of these action oriented teenagers when they felt it was not enough to keep observing and commenting on problems and solutions. Instead, they made up their minds to get to the act and actually build something to address the issues and opportunities they could sense in the immediate physical as well as virtual world around them. "We always wanted to be entrepreneurs," Sanjay adds with retrospection, "and the best thing to build our enterprise around would have been the one thing that we are both equally and sincerely passionate about, that is coding!"

This streak of entrepreneurial exploration is what led the young siblings to start coding for simple and yet effective applications that were based on basic utilities. However, once they started observing their own efficiency and the kind of approving response they were getting from the user base they had, they decided to take the next step and give their passion a more formal and organized shape. This took a more constructive form when the duo decided to start working as a collective unit – a company registered in their names instead of simply working as two individual coders.

"It obviously made a lot of sense for us since we had been working together so we decided to become co-founders of a company under which we could take more concrete steps in the field of digital development," Shravan shares.

Walking back and forth from school, the boys would discuss how and when and what their enterprise would comprise of, and what they would call it. Amidst all these discussions, decisions and deliberations, one thing was crystal clear to the young, soon-to-be partners that they would have equal stakes, equal inputs and equal participation in whatever they did together.

"When it came to choosing the name for the venture, we were both stuck with our individual choices. It was actually quite funny since we had almost reached a dead end!" Sanjay exclaims. While Sanjay, with the actionable drive, wanted to pursue the word 'go' for the enterprise, Shravan wanted a diverse approach and was hooked to the word 'dimensions'.

"You know sometimes you have clear signs that symbolize a lot more than simply appears. The naming of our company was just one of those. As individuals, we were stuck with words that were somewhat incomplete, but as a team, we formed a pair that is incredibly complementary," Shravan reflects, "thus we came together in our decision to name the venture GoDimensions. Today the word stands for not only everything we want to reach but also signifies the team effort in everything we do."

I have to pinch myself to come back to eality that the dynamic persons I am talking to are really two school going kids who have just come back from their classes. A quick look around their rooms reveals an elaborately placed Xbox – something they both swear by and are often found lounging with when they are not busy with other things. Also found in the room are their toys, a massive poster of Lionel Messi, the legendary Argentinian football player and their work cum study desks. It is a strange amalgamation to see course books, notepads, planners and work designs in a montage together in the room and lives of these exceptionally talented and versatile boys. Sitting on a stool, talking and smiling his teenage smile, Shravan suddenly picks up a guitar and starts strumming a popular tune with the effortlessness of an artist.

Is there something these boys cannot do? I wonder with sheep-eyed adoration. However, watching all this come into play before my eyes also validates the reflection that if one has the drive and the will to step up, nothing else really matters.

"I don't want to sound arrogant but there's only so much that educational qualifications and professional experiences can credit for your motivation. Ultimately, it all boils down to how strongly you feel about something and what you are willing to do to overcome your fears and make your dreams come true."

I cannot believe I am hearing these words out of a sixteen-year-old's mouth. But then again, this has been a day to shake all my notions of what it takes to make it big.

It is within these walls that the brothers have observed, ideated and implemented their plans and built some of the most astonishing applications with the simplicity that only a high degree of insight and expertise can deliver. From applications for emergency contact for elders and people in distress, to gaming applications, from education based games to very complex automated security applications, this duo has built and sold a series of extremely successful and highly acclaimed applications that have made it big not only in the Indian scenario but have found their fan base all over the world.

"Most of our products are based on everyday necessities and situations. What happens if you are away and don't want to leave behind your keys with the neighbors? What happens if an elderly person needs emergency health services and has no one to turn to?" These are some of the situations you encounter on a day to day basis. This is what we work for – digital solutions that will make the world a better place," Shravan explains.

It has indeed been a path of steady success for GoDimensions with the aim it has set out to achieve. And why wouldn't that be true? As firm believers in doing good, the brothers speak in earnest about their ambition to make this generation of mobi-sapiens as evolved and efficient in the best way possible, in due consideration and respect of one's environment. Which is why, perhaps, that as astonishing as their technological accomplishment has been, what impresses the world even more is the sensitivity and maturity with which these young minds have been progressing in their ambition.

"At the current stage, it is not our aim to make money or become an aggressively competitive company," Sanjay shares, "Our immediate goal is to set the foundation, to build a base and learn as much as we can about the waters we are sailing into."

Having said that, however, the enterprise is already making a sufficient amount of money through ads on their, otherwise free to use, downloadable applications.

As if one needed monitory evaluation to describe the success of the siblings anyway! None the less, there is no dearth of appreciation and recognition that has followed Shravan and Sanjay from the very beginning of their endeavours. From being featured on every single newspaper at local and national platforms, to being covered in short videos by some of the most prime news channels of the country, from making it as the front news content across different digital media in verticals of start-ups, business, innovation or technology, to being critically acclaimed by many of the stalwarts in the country and the world, the brothers have already been there and done that. Some of the most reputed colleges are known to have invited the young co-founders for inspirational talks to several cities in the world. They have addressed panels in conferences, delivered talks to professionals, and even been invited for conversations to other parts of the world as motivational speakers and inspiring entrepreneurs.

"Imagine a couple of teenagers addressing a hall full of experts, aspirants and simply even elders!" Shravan exclaims. "That's how intimidating the experiences have been. But they have been truly nerve bending, extremely inspiring and incredibly comforting to be there, to watch people nod in support and appreciation; this is what makes us feel that we are on the right track!"

Some might wonder what it does to the personal life of these budding leaders of the world. Some are even concerned about whether they are growing up too fast. But one quick look into their lives and you will know that this is the most natural course of action for them, and they lead pretty ordinary days in their extraordinary manner.

"Our primary hours are spent in school. After that, we come home, get some rest, finish our home work and study what we have to. It is then that we open up our assigned tasks for GoDimensions for the day and dedicate our energy in ideating, brainstorming or coding," Sanjay reveals. Between being the master minds behind a successfully rising enterprise and leading their school lives, the brothers also find time to jam, play on their Xbox and even hang out with friends outdoors. With complete support from their parents, the brothers have been brought up in an environment that has taught them to explore new possibilities fearlessly and yet be mindful of all the resources available to them as a privilege.

"Our father is our biggest supporter and our biggest critic too. He is the one who funds our projects or any investment we might need for new encounters. However, it's not that easy to impress him," Shravan shakes his head with a grin, "we have to make an influential pitch and convince him that his investment is a good value for money."

At an age when most boys are still struggling with their emotional issues or throwing tantrums about buying crazy trendy things, the brothers have left me awestruck with their insightful and yet simplistic understanding of life.

It is also a reflection of their personal equation with one another that blossoms as a result of their journey. One of the biggest reasons that GoDimensions is what it is today is because the siblings have had each other to fall back on.

"We are companions in many ways. As brothers, we are compatible and trusting, as same-aged boys, we click on the same issues and as entrepreneurs, we explore different sides of the same coin that helps us build together a strong and holistic product," Sanjay and Shravan share in unison. While the elder brother is more dedicated towards the technical nuances of the product, the younger sibling dedicates his knowledge towards user experience. The result is a product impeccable in its technology and smooth in its utility. This is what perhaps keeps them amidst the best ranked application builders. The key lies in their insight and simplicity – a flawless combination which is hard to find even in the most experienced entities. With this critical combination, the brothers have also been growing in the past few years towards more strength and respect for each other's capacity. Not only are their decisions always mutual and considerate towards each other's opinions but the fact that they stick together despite the name and fame is a good sign for the duo.

As I take my leave and thank the boys for their time, I watch them sit by the window and continue strumming music on the guitar – perhaps one of their regular jamming sessions has just begun. It might be a little too soon to tell what roads are yet to be taken for these astounding brothers cum entrepreneurs, it is safe to say that it will definitely be a high road, one that will inspire and shape many simple and yet powerful functions of the world. I leave these questions to imagination and enjoy the little melody still playing in the background, their energy still inspiring me with the magnanimous dimensions that the young entrepreneurs have already begun to explore.

GoDimensions For interesting apps and more, visit www.godimensions.com and Twitter: @AppGodimensions.

*Sisters **Fidan** (right) and **Ezan** (left) transformed their love for trendy footwear to a fruitful startup with **Head Over Heels**, which makes available chic footwear at affordable prices.*

Breaking All Rules

Head Over Heels by Fidan & Ezan

Who says it takes luxury to buy happiness? Who says that only solitaire dreams find platinum realities? And whoever says it takes years to ripen in this big wide world, I am not even considering that a valid enough point. If you notice the system of the world, you will observe that there are these stoic set of rules that the people of the world seem to have made, although nobody knows who exactly made them. These set of rules are not written anywhere, nobody speaks them out loud but deep down in our growing up environment, no matter where we are in the world, the seeds of these rules are instructionally embedded and condition us into believing them, forbidding us to challenge them. Rules like 'you need to be educated to make it big in life', or 'it has to be pricey to be good!' or even that to be taken seriously you need a bunch of years (which most certainly you have no role to play in, because time is linear and you will, after all, keep growing older by virtue of inertia!) to your credit to be taken seriously. In this big wide world, most of us do not question these rules or even remotely try to understand the source and logic behind them. Only a choicest few will ever rise up to wonder what happens on the other side of these veils of rules. And it is in the rarest of the rare cases that someone discards these rules to undo the belief system set around it, go ahead and rework the mechanism, and lo and behold, they recreate their world without these set of rules (or any set of rules for that matter) and emerge victorious warriors. These instances are so rare and so unique that when you come across such instances, you should quickly grab your thinking cap, a bunch of questions to satiate your inquisitiveness and an address book to track down the legends, just as I did. Only even more astounding in this case was the fact that these dynamite people, instead of the stereotypical warrior-like image of men, are actually women, or honestly speaking, young girls really, who have been shaking the foundation of what the world agrees upon.

In the small city of Calicut of the Indian state Kerala, a place I can bet a lot of people will not be able to pin on a map, two young girls who have just stepped into the early side of their twenties, were going on their usual lives in pursuit of happiness. This meant that after having successfully completed their schooling, they were now attending college. Enaz Rafiq pursuing her degree in Bachelors in Commerce and simultaneously also had managed to complete the second level of Company Secretary exam. It was now her turn to study and complete the final year of CS to then be able to pick up a stable, lucrative job, as expected by her parents and the society. Fidan, a year junior to Enaz, was also busy at this stage in studying in the same city, pursuing her Bachelor's degree in Business Administration. How the two chanced upon each other's life is no mystery and frankly, they didn't have a lot of role to play in this because they were born into the same family, as sisters with a gap of only one year of age. However, what they made out of this stroke of fate was entirely up to them.

They could either go on living as two ordinary siblings, with a simple bond of blood, growing up to be individuals with separate lives, or they could make the most of what the gift of similar DNA had brought to them. It was a gift of dedicated passion, of compatibility beyond comparison and it was a liking towards similar things. And be certain that they managed to avail this opportunity in the strangest and most incredible way possible. But first let us tune back to what happened within the family at the beginning of this incredulous journey.

"It all started at the dinner table. Fidan and I were discussing a collection of shoes we had seen in the market and we both were talking about how even we can create better shoe designs than that," Enaz recollects chirpily. The sisters are known to have a very similar and passionate taste in fashion from a very young age. Even as kids, they would mix and match their clothes and borrow whatever their mother would lend them for the sake of their experiments. It is here that their fetish for shoes found new dimensions and thus began the journey that led them to explore different kinds of footwear, experiment with what was available into what could be made swankier. Thus, the dinner table conversation that Enaz was referring to was a commonplace conversation for both the sisters to discuss the make, design, style and cost of some or the other footwear they had chanced upon. Even their parents, who were by now accustomed to these conversations, took it to be the usual chitter-chatter between the sisters. Except that as it would turn out, this wasn't meant to be ordinary chitter-chatter.

From commenting on available designs in the market, the conversation steered towards the kind of price tags these designs had and this was followed by the casual declaration by the sisters that they could definitely do a better job of making better shoes. This led to calculations from the top of their heads to see how they would pitch these imaginary shoes in terms of pricing and marketing positioning.

"They're off to one of their dreamy castles again!" Their mother would have possibly thought. The only difference this time was that the conversation did not stay limited to dreams, and amidst those bouts of laughter, jokes, dreams and discussions, somewhere the sisters found this a plan building inside them that would materialize into reality.

"As long as it was limited to the dinner table, we probably would have taken it as a joke ourselves. But when we found ourselves talking about it even more seriously the following day, with ideas and suggestions bubbling in our heads about the nitty-gritties, I think it was safe to say that we really were going to give this a shot!" Fidan exclaims.

And thus, at the age of twenty one and twenty respectively, Ezan and Fidan set out on the path of converting their undying confession of love for footwear into making footwear that the world could fall in love with. It didn't take long for the sisters to figure out what, how and where they would convert this idea into reality.

"The process was simple, we would make footwear for college going girls, like ourselves. The taste and tone would be swanky, one that goes with the funky college wear for the young and fashionable girls. The most important factor would be its pricing, where it would be pitched at an affordable rate so that the target audience could afford these pairs to go with whatever they were wearing."

The girls had basically built a dream that they wanted to see come true for girls just like them who enjoyed equal love for funky footwear and cared about the kind of price they were paying for it.

"The beginning was pretty hilarious. We decided to test our market by making a page on Facebook to showcase some of our work and introduce the funky designs we were offering at the pricing under rupees five hundred," Fidan shares. The results were astonishing! Overnight, they had begun receiving requests, queries and orders on the basis of the attractive designs and creative outlay.

"It was something that people of Calicut had never seen before and the best part was that it was at a price that was turning out to be a great deal!" With the unique selling point of their price at under 499, the sisters were hitting the right nerve amongst their audience that wanted fashion and wanted it cheap. With the kind of response that was knocking at their door, the duo pitched their idea to their parents who were both flabbergasted and impressed all at once. "It was amazing of them to humor us. After all, it was our simple fetish we were trying to feed and they were sure we would let it go in some time," Ezan jokes. "We were genuinely encouraged by them to experiment with our interests but there was only one condition. We were asked to not compromise with our education and this could carry on for as long as we wanted."

With these basics in place, they set out to look for a place to set up their work place. With no capital to begin with, they were evidently wary of investing right away.

"Like cautious, first time entrepreneurs, we did not want to dive in head first with expenses without first testing our sustainability," Fidan speaks in retrospection. It was at this stage that they ultimately began their office in the spandrel under the staircase. With a family who had confidence in the daughters and above all, shared love to help their dreams come true, the siblings were blessed with the support of their father who made the initial investment to help the girls kick start operation. With this, a gorgeous, princess-y, pink store was launched in the city of Calicut under the banner of 'Head Over Heels' which was a true reflection of the passionate love that the sisters shared for footwear and that which they were certain would also be the sentiment of all the young college girls when they were introduced to this swanky new range.

As dreamers turned entrepreneurs, the creative sisters have come a long way from under the staircase and speak knowingly of their business idea. "The market in Calicut had a decent collection for the seekers of jewelry and salwars. In terms of footwear, there were a few showrooms of the standard, popular brands but they came with hefty price tags and only the commonly set trends of foot fashion," Ezan speaks reflecting on the business opportunity. But there was no respite for people seeking chic but yet cheap options. The sisters could completely relate with the dearth and understood how their peers would rejoice if such an outlet came to their rescue. "All we had to do was club this incredible business opportunity with our skill and interest. And viola, Head Over Heels became an instant hit!" she cheers.

With four years of operation, Ezan and Fidan are proud owners of four gorgeous and popular stores of Head Over Heels and thousands of fans and followers today. And this base of exemplary creativity and strength is only growing bigger and better. "Honestly, we thought that HOH would carry on for two or three years at the most while we were still pursuing our education. I couldn't have imagined that we would come such a long way to sustain and expand so miraculously," Fidan confesses in all earnestness. But a long way they did come with support, appreciation and respect earned not only in the family but also their target audience. Within the first year of operation, the sisters had already been featured in all the major television and print channels of media. With over fifty interviews broadcasted on national and international platforms, Head Over Heels has certainly made its presence felt in the world of fashion entrepreneurs. "I can't describe to you the feeling of such recognition. I mean it is one thing to have some acknowledgement in your neighborhood. But when a reputed newspaper prints a half page article in your name, a feat for which big brands pay an insane amount of money, you know you're on the right track to make it big!" Ezan shares.

The sisters have walked this path together with mutual respect and cooperation. Through this unplanned and unexpected journey, they have figured out the way to make it click. "What really helps as partners is that we really think alike. I know it is a rarity amongst siblings," Fidan jokes, "but with the same interests, passion and aspiration, it helps us stay in sync with one another." Admitting that although conflicts come up on rare occasions, the siblings explain that they are always open to differences as it helps them add more diversity and spice to the enterprise. To make matters simpler, they have divided the responsibility of two stores each between themselves and make the best of their individual as well as collective capacity to bring out the best of their venture. "We make individual contributions and respect each other's space. But at the same time, we involve each other in decisions, suggestions and innovations. It is a critical balance that I think you can attain with only someone you share a close bond with. I guess we are just very lucky to have this natural partnership in whatever we are doing together," says Ezan.

If you wonder how realistic this culmination of dreams has been for the sisters, all you have to do step into their stores or catch up with the siblings while they are at their stores and you will see that the simplistic breakdown with which they have made this idea into a reality is so practical that you can't help being in awe.

"We now know of many ventures that have copied our styles, even began under staircases and gone as far as taken 'inspiration' from our creative range," Fidan shares. "While on one hand, this goes on to establish our fan following, really flattering to an extent to know that we can 'inspire' people to follow suit. It is also true that, at the risk of sounding vain, we can safely say that we have a cutting edge with our creativity and pricing advantage that make us both practical as well as undoubted favorites amidst people who loyally love us."

They did not have the right set of degrees for a fashion range, neither did they have the list of experience with the known names on their resumes to speak for. To make matters worse, they were just a couple of young college going girls from a simple background. In short, they would have appeared to you as a combination of everything ordinary, fitting into a certain set of rules in the world. But it was their passion, their determination and their undying support for each other that brought them to break the chains of these rules, to de-establish every single rule that the world has set for people to make it big. Even today, as a signing off comment, the words of the sisters leave me spellbound and in perfect belief of their conviction when I ask them what would they have done if HOH didn't work. "Something else, anything incredible, together as sisters and partners. And this, we would have done with our heads held high knowing that we had given our best to make our dream come true." With aims to grow, dream bigger and fly higher, Fidan and Ezan continue to make shoes and news and have earned far more than what mere money in an enterprise can make. They have earned awe, respect and a bond between sisters that will help them rule their world.

 For classy footwear that's easy on the pocket, visit their store in Calicut, Kannur or Cochin, or follow them on Facebook:/headoverheelscalicut.

Siblings **Rahul** *(left) and* **Swati** *(right) started up an online portal named* **IndustryBuying** *to enable hassle-free buying of industrial tools and supplies.*

The Industrious Genesis

IndustryBuying by Rahul & Swati

Most people in the world follow conventions. There are set paths in every domain that the league of ordinary people will follow. These are safe tracks, based on experiences of other people or negations laid down with guidelines of things forbidden or fears of failures induced. Most people abide by these guidelines for they do not know better. Most people are told not to dare. For most people, there is no one waiting and standing behind them, encouraging them to take the first bold steps and find out for themselves. For most people, there is no one who understands their dreams and believes in them. That is one of the primary reasons why most people don't dream and even those who dream do not dare.

In the world of entrepreneurs, the silver line between dreaming and daring comes with a prominent challenge. With fast increasing opportunities and connections all over the world, many people are exposed to the viability of creating their own enterprise or breaking the conventional paths to make way for something more self-motivated. However, the baggage of traditional notions of normative and the pressure of stability in a career choice include some of the biggest factors that control these viabilities. While some of these apprehensions and fears hold true and find

101

validation in experiences and failures that people have experienced in the past, they also pose as some of the biggest hindrances in the path of those who want to achieve more than what the normative can afford. Sometimes, despite having all that it takes to make the extraordinary work, people fail in their dreams, or worse, do not even work on making these dreams come true for the simple reason that they lack the subtle yet critical nudge to get things rolling. In this racy and competitive world, it is a challenge to find people who want to whole heartedly and sincerely support you in realizing these dreams.

But why must we talk about that? Because we know that deep inside each one of us, are ideas that are desperate to blossom, there are barriers we want to cross over and explorations we crave to make. But these are all the things that the big wise world has taught us not to do because it is dangerous and may possibly lead to failure. It is in scenarios like these that one wonders what the chances would have been if instead of the voices of all the nay-sayers in the world, were echoes of support, encouragement and perhaps even companionship to actualize the dreams? Would that reduce the risks involved? Would that magically transform one's limitations and make one omnipotent? Most likely not! However, would this provide the strength to walk through the storm? Would this bring the relief of having someone watching your back? Most probably, yes!

Back in the days when India was still alien to the platform of e-commerce and was as stubborn against online purchase reliability as kids are against entering dark alleys, B2B transactions were all happening in offline models. Not only was this a major challenge to scaling but also required a lot more tedious demand and supply strategies and monitoring. Lack of faith in an online model coupled with the habitual purchase experience with only direct transactions were some of the major challenges being encountered. It is no surprise then that very few people even looked in the direction of ecommerce when it came to planning new ventures.

It was in these critically challenging times that Swati and Rahul had been gathering efficiency and experience in the business domain, understanding the basic mechanisms and evaluating the marketing pattern at national as well as international platforms. Having acquired her education in science and finance at bachelor's and master's level, Swati moved to the United States for consultancy in a reputed organization where she was exposed to a range of business platforms with different models and capacities. Rahul, on the other hand, had pursued his education in the discipline of science and was also working in America and aggressively involved with Wall Street. Having handled and understood the business vertical at an international level, Rahul had also grasped the nuances of entrepreneurial foundation. It was then that he decided to leave the comforts of his cushioned job, come back to India and handle his family business of industrial distribution. It was also around this time that Swati was given the responsibility to handle the Indian segment of her firm's business. This may be labelled as a stroke of luck or perhaps an excuse that was meant to bring the Swati and Rahul back together again. After all, they did have a history together.

Rahul and Swati are known to many as the inseparable siblings, partners in crime and two ends of a string, owing to their relentless and yet extremely opposing bond with each other. Like most siblings, it is their differences that makes them both fight and love each other. Perhaps, it is also these differences that have brought them to an entirely new level of partnership with each other, one that has developed beyond their personal equation and on to a platform of professional dynamics. After their respective stints, the duo combined their efforts and interests together to follow the calling of their professional path and rerouted to work in the direction of business, just like their parents had been building for decades.

However, unlike the conventional paths taken by prodigies of families in business, the brother-sister duo set out to dare the unheard and make space in the virtual market by providing an extensive range of business and industrial products to SMEs as well as large businesses through an online portal. Thus, in the year 2013, the Indian e-commerce saw the birth of IndustryBuying – the joint venture of Swati and Rahul, that was created to redesign the organization, or the lack of it, in the domain of industrial product procurement.

"Having worked in the international space with some of the best business designs of the world, coming back to India revealed to us a challenge glaring in our faces; there was absolutely no platform for organized demand and supply for industrial buying," Swati reveals. It was this challenge that prompted the duo to channelize all their experience into the right direction and make the best of this opportunity.

The idea to start something of their own struck as the most natural choice; an instinct that comes as a family trait. Hailing from a family that runs its own business, the siblings, even as young adults were taught and told about the nuances of the world of enterprise. It was therefore no surprise for the family when Rahul and Swati turned to creating their own venture.

"You know it is always a tough decision to quit on your stable lucrative job to start something different from the conventional – especially if it involves something as unpredictable and out of the box as an e-commerce portal," explains Rahul in retrospection, "but our parents were so unconditionally supportive and encouraged us from the very first stage; that was the source of our motivation."

That the duo would steer in this direction was but natural. But that they should turn to each other on this path of adventure was unpredictable and yet, in a way, the most auriferous decision to make.

"When the decision to start this online portal was made, there were a lot of major and minor things to resolve. But the biggest of all these resolutions, and I would call it the most critical one, was that we would partner up with this venture," Rahul speaks. Out of the many challenges a rising entrepreneur experiences through the phase of genesis, one of the most testing decision is who will be your leaning pillar cum partner in this journey. Many turn to best friends, colleagues, sometimes, even life-partners in this course. But few dare to tread the waters with their own siblings. With the obvious stakes, one would think this fear to be justified, but this pair seems to contradict this belief in both their words and actions.

"We have grown up together, facing the same kind of challenges. We have also seen each other through thick and thin. Despite whatever relations we have with the rest of the world, including our parents or spouses, we are the go-to person for each other in good times and bad," Swati shares candidly about her equation with her supportive brother.

Once this major decision was made, the duo toiled together, lucubrating through all forms of market research and understanding to build their B2B e-commerce portal. With the goal and methodology clear in their heads, they launched IndustryBuying with its straightforward impression – reflecting its straightforward mission and nature, that is, to facilitate a platform for industrial buying. Catering to both e-trading and enterprises, IndustryBuying not only secured itself as the first B2B e-commerce portal in the country but has also managed to bring itself into a position of appreciable recognition and wide user-ship from across diverse industrial domains in the country.

Although looking at the current situation of IndustryBuying, one may be tempted to think that the siblings had it all figured out, having the silver spoon of a family business background and so on, but that would be a mistake people with a superficial perspective could easily make. Like any starting enterprise, the siblings' venture also experienced its days of trials before walking the glory road.

"There was a time when our consumer bank was not even in double digits. With limited buyers linked to us, sometimes, the number of orders would not even reach ten in a day. These were the times when to keep our morale high and stay in faith was a tenacious challenge," Rahul reveals with humble honesty.

With the lack of initial funds, advertising and resource building was also a hurdle that the brother-sister duo had to boot-strap through their initial phase. However, success doesn't shy for long from those who pursue it sagaciously. After securing their series A funding, the tables turned for the duo and within six months of that, they even managed to secure their second – a nine million funding. It was then that the true aggressive form of sales and revamping of their e-commerce website took a ride. Ever since then, there has been no looking back for the pair. It was when a few enterprise customers such as Hindustan Unilever, Havells, Bombardier, Motherson Sumi, Escorts and others started procuring industrial utility products directly from IndustryBuying that the siblings heaved a breath of relief as their landmark of true accomplishment. They even began extending their presence aggressively in the tier two and tier three cities, a course that had so far been difficult for them because they did not have the luxury of that kind of expansion or reach.

Having started from scratch, with no Indian model to look up to, no lessons to observe and learn from, and no ground proof to pitch to the investors, Rahul and Swati have brought their venture a long way. They began with a team growing from six to ten members – a consortium selected on the stringent criteria of passion and dedication among people who were willing to invest their skills in an idea relatively alien to the Indian set-up. Today, the family of IndustryBuying stands at an astounding 500-member strength with a footprint around 21,000 pin codes across the nation.

"You would think that the metropolitans and the so-called forward cities of the country would be the most progressive in adapting to the e-commerce culture. But surprisingly, our major costumer share comes from B and C cities and towns," Swati shares with excitement. This goes on to reveal the amazing opportunity that the siblings have managed to tap on and even more so, succeeded in penetrating effectively through a variety of domain and geography.

They say that it doesn't matter how tall a tree shoots, what keeps its spine erect is the root that binds its strength. A similar notion is also true for Swati and Rahul in their professional endeavour. That they have the backing of a family to support and encourage them would be an understatement to make. Not only have they received the erudite words and experiences from the learned members of the family, but also received encouragement in ideas that members of the older generation may or may not have related to in this new age world of technology.

"It is interesting to see the business spirit of old and new age conglomerate into one another. While instincts and buying principles remain the same, the methodology and channels have evolved. You should hear our conversations at the dining table; it seems like the melting point of two worlds!" Rahul jokes. But what he reveals in this light humored manner is perhaps one of the biggest secrets that has kept the siblings rooted and together through the challenges of their business's evolution. Furthermore, it is also the Sisyphean support of their respective spouses that has brought them the strength and relief to take the leaps of faith they need in the path of their adventure ride.

"It makes a big difference to know that someone is counting on you and at the same time holds immense confidence in your capacity; I think this is one of the biggest reasons that keep both Rahul and me motivated in the long run!" Swati explains with passionate insight.

No matter what people might think about the threats and troubles of partnering up with a sibling, Rahul and Swati have gone on to redefine the dimensions of what sibling-hood means to them. They have made the best of their bond, their strengths and understanding of each other in the professional domain and proved to be a pillar of strength for each other.

"One of the biggest virtues of our equation is that we complement each other so perfectly; this has really helped to define the kind of roles and responsibilities we have assumed in the enterprise," Swati explains.

With the extensive experience she has had in roles that have enhanced her leadership skills, Swati is a pro when it comes to handling that side of her own business. Rahul, on the other hand, has handled so many collaborations at the business end and strengthened his networking skills over the years. Thus, he handles these aspects for IndustryBuying. With this perfectly mutual understanding and respect for talent, the siblings manage to not over-step each other's roles but also excel in making the best of what each sets out to do, and in helping the other out wherever advice is sought. But beyond the work-force equation that this entrepreneurial journey has churned for them, it is also the depths of personal trust, understanding and respect that the duo has experienced for each other which have helped to enhance their personal equation beyond comparison.

"No matter what we do, where we are or whatever we are dealing with, it is this incessant support that we hold for each other that gives us our biggest strength; what more could you ask for in a relationship with your sibling?" Swati shares emotionally. For the many budding entrepreneurs of the country, the insightful advice of Rahul also echoes his sister's comments,

"You need to put your ego and fears aside; that's all that is needed in an equation with your sibling. They can be your closest friend, guide and critic."

With reflections of mutual admiration and a compatibility to be envious of, Swati and Rahul get back to taking their calls and responding to emails, almost in sync with each other's mood and energy. It is no doubt that the mechanism of this industrious duo is destined to create a hallmark of success and inspire many siblings in the country to dare and follow suit.

Brother-sister duo **Abhishek** *(left) and* **Arushi** *(right) kick-started* **KreateKonnect** *to provide every seller the best e-commerce tools, and innovative ideas backed with modern technology.*

Creating an Entrepreneurial Connection

KreateKonnect by Abhishek & Arushi

Some people are strong believers in destiny and positivity and propagate that success comes to those who earn it and hold faith that whatever they do, they will make the best of the circumstances. It is not only extraordinary tasks that go into the making of big people but also extraordinary beliefs and conviction that work at a level that is beyond simple reason and comprehension. The inherent philosophy of 'we are what we think', initiated by Buddha has come a long way in hand with some of the most efficient examples of good thoughts that have led to great actions. In times when our confidence is shaken, beliefs put in turmoil or self-esteem at stake, one must simply remember that wanting something innately, sincerely and virtuously and reading the signs that the universe presents to us is the ultimate solution to cracking even the biggest hurdles of life. No matter how gigantic a challenge may seem, no matter if it is in the personal sphere or professional domain, no matter whether it is about individual battles of relationship qualms, resolutions of the self and determinations can cross all boundaries – that is the secret.

One experiences this in the subtle or gross levels through life in ways that are sometimes explicit and sometimes revealed only in sequence of results. Such is the story of the siblings Abhishek and Arushi who have put their complete faith and commitment into what they believed, and hence turned things around them to convert challenges into opportunities. It was the sheer pursuit of their passion that encouraged the duo to step out of their comfort zone and discover their own spaces, albeit with the strong support of each other. Both Arushi and her elder sibling have an education in business administration, and have been eminently exhibiting their inclination towards entrepreneurial diocese. While Abhishek pursued a professional growth chart with some of the most reputed banks in the country, he earned a deep and critical understanding of business management from end to end. This also helped to enhance his understanding of financial administration. It was after a series of such experiences that he was drawn towards the idea of building something of his own to put his business expertise to use in an independent and creative enterprise. Thus, the idea and then the seeds of an innovative platform of e-commerce was brought to life after incessant brainstorming and organization of Abhishek and his business partner, Piyush who has ever since stuck with Abhishek and helped to strengthen the foundations of the start-up. Arushi, on the other hand has had her share of experience working in the corporate sector and gathered the nuances of organizational intricacies. However, when she got married, Arushi had to shift base to the city of Jaipur and was in search of opportunities to restart her career flow at the new location. It was then that her adoring and encouraging brother nudged her to come on-board with the enterprise and find her own space to explore and strengthen as a part of the organization. Thus began the journey of Arushi and Abhishek as professional siblings apart from being a close-knit duo by birth.

Their entrepreneurial journey began with innovation in the online trading industry, assessing the market opportunity.

"Our mission is to provide result oriented e-commerce solutions to domestic sellers and link their products to the audiences worldwide. Thus, we enable sellers and our business partners to excel in the e-economy and enliven the brand," Abhishek explains.

With this intention, the brain child of Abhishek and his friend cum partner Piyush, came into existence by the name of Kreate Konnect.

"The name of our company summarizes exactly what we do. We Kreate a suitable platform for our clients by providing them best end to end e-commerce solutions enabling them to sell their products across the globe and Konnecting them and bringing them at par with the world," Arushi shares drawing from the innovative name of the enterprise.

Her involvement after the genesis of the enterprise came through the support and encouragement, coupled by Arushi's own enthusiasm to explore the unconventional territory of the world of enterprise.

"Ever since I was a child I was used to discussing every little detail with my brother. Like every other sibling, we too have had many fights, we have been at each other's throat some zillion times but that didn't change our affection or my equation to fall back on him for advice," Arushi shares candidly.

It was during one of these candid conversations with her brother that Arushi was intrigued with the idea of joining his business to convert her interests into a professional dimension. With this privilege and support system, her role was defined as per her interest and location. "Since I am based in Jaipur and it's a hub for manufacturers I acquired the role of the curator. I always had a thing to find new innovative things to gift to my family member or to find unique things for use at home; this passion helped me a lot to define my role in the company."

This acumen as a growing adult, complemented with her experience with HNI customers has truly helped her in communicating effectively with the prospective and existing clients, and execute the policies of Kreate Konnect efficiently. It is her contributions that have helped them find associates for the business who sell innovative products and are keen on co-branding with the enterprise.

Abhishek, on the other hand, has always been interested in digital marketing. From hunting down various sources of services on the e-commerce portals, to finding the best deals, offers and most efficient amenities that connect various B2B and B2C platforms, Abhishek was on it from a very young stage. In fact, it was this interest that got him famous amongst family and friends as the go-to person for suggestions or advice on any online features.

"It is his strong belief and passion that got him to choose his direction of profession. I have to say, that *bhaiya* (Abhishek) has been very lucky to be able to follow his interest as his career. Perhaps that's the reason why he can stay so dedicated and successful in what he chose to follow," Arushi shares ecstatically.

Having built the idea from scratch with Piyush, Abhishek has used the best of his experiences and learning and invested wisely into the venture. It is in this process that he has sought and employed the help of his devoted and talented sister to support him in business development. "We are both in sync with each other's thoughts and actions. That is one of the most important reasons why we decided to work with each other," Abhishek revels in his equation with his younger sibling. It is the utilization of both their skills and understanding that has gotten them into this professional equation.

"People say that professional relations between people are often the biggest reasons to spoil the personal equations. However, in our case, it is the compatibility and comfort that we share in the personal sphere that helps us to strengthen our professional bond," he adds insightfully.

"It is one of the most efficient platforms I have seen that caters to my business needs. To be able to reach an audience at this scale is exactly what I needed."

There are many such feedbacks from entrepreneurs who have joined Kreate Konnect either as channeling partners or selling brands that have sought and achieved success through this fast expanding start-up. This, along with the fast growing user-base and the rising popularity of the enterprise across different channels of the media, are clear signs that Kreate Konnect has made its own mark in the space of e-commerce in the Indian as well as international market. With further plans of aggressive expansions, the siblings have been trying all the old and new mechanisms to strengthen their position in the domain. Obviously, competition from different sources is prominent and equally innovative. Hence, to say that their scenario is easy and smooth, or has been from the beginning would be far removed from reality.

"We have seen our share of challenges from the advent of Kreate Konnect, or should I say, even at the stage of ideation," Abhishek speaks in retrospect. In the initial stage, the siblings bootstrapped the enterprise and limited their expenses to the most minimal needs. "I have seen the struggle from the beginning. On one hand, one doesn't have enough funds to invest in marketing or resources. On the other hand, in the aggressive market space and the challenge to make yourself noticeable, financial strength stands as one of the strongest pillars of support," Arushi comments with experience. However, judicious decisions and meticulous appropriation of the resources helped them to achieve a stability and efficiency that is inspiration worthy. It was also a challenge to bring together a team who could identify their dedication and understanding with the siblings.

"When Kreate Konnect started kicking up in scale and success, we started expanding our team beyond the core members. This was one of the biggest challenges because to be able to find people with skills may not be as difficult, but to find people with the passion to work with limited resources and to think of the organization as their own, that is what is a true encounter," Abhishek shares from the experience of the past.

However, from two friends ideating a business model to setting up the entire enterprise, Kreate Konnect has definitely come a long way. With the current staff of twenty-five steadfast members, the venture has been achieving milestones with consistent development. Overcoming the initial scarcity, when acquiring even a single client would seem to be a herculean task, the siblings have worked upwards to connecting hundreds of customers and enterprises from across domains through an efficient and effective network of collaborations.

While relations with the external and entrepreneurial face has been developing steadily, standing tall through the tests of time, the relationship status between the siblings has also been strengthening through these years of association.

"After my marriage, while the hunt for a career opportunity occupied a lot of my attention, it was also a genuine concern for my family and I that the work I find should be both of my interest and also be reliable," Arushi shares, "thus when I decided to join my brother in his business, not only was it a welcome move for everyone, but also a relief for my parents because they knew this was a reliable association."

The balance between personal and professional relations is what helps the duo understand each other and share a comfort zone which helps their progress. In businesses between friends or family, it not uncommon for power play and ego clashes to bring up walls between personal relations and professional equations. When ideas differ or roles interfere, it leads to the downfall of even the most promising opportunities.

"I can see why people have apprehensions about working with their siblings; after all, you have practically fought all your life with them, why would you take that kind of a risk?" Abhishek unfolds the mystery of his collaboration with Arushi by elaborating on the ease with which they have chosen their own roles and responsibilities in the venture.

As ambitious and articulate people, the duo has been able to explore and express their areas of interest with absolute conviction and hence been able to choose their respective domains.

"We have never had to contest amidst us for hierarchy," Arushi reveals.

Since the duo has given themselves the time and freedom to explore and choose what they love to do, they are not only extremely comfortable in the roles they have taken up but also strive to make the best of every challenge and opportunity for a holistic growth of Kreate Konnect in general.

"We don't have boundaries of what is my role or his role. Although we have respective designations, but our equation is such that we move beyond these definitions and try to contribute in any way for the best interest of the enterprise." The siblings echo this sentiment equally. If you think that they would deliberately try to keep a delicate distance between their personal and professional borders, the brother sister duo begs to disagree.

"We honestly do not have these home and work boundaries. Our entrepreneurial passion keeps us ideating and contemplating about new developments no matter what we are doing or where we are. When you're so dedicated to something, it no longer remains 'work' but really becomes your life!" Abhishek speaks with a passion that betrays his ambitious acumen.

It is also perhaps this dedication that the duo feels about Kreate Konnect that encourages them to share all big and small ideas with each other with candid enthusiasm.

"It is not like my brother and I don't have differences in our opinions. There are times when we think differently about different things. But the endeavour is always to bring diverse ideas and understanding to the table and to make the best of deliberations for the interest of our organization," Arushi shares insightfully.

Rising from strong belief and optimism, the siblings have come a really long way into creating opportunities and mapping their own track of success. Not only have Abhishek and Arushi defied conventions, overcome their apprehensions and left their cushioned lives to put everything at stake for this enterprise, but also stood up together against the most challenging circumstances to support and encourage each other in this precarious and yet rewarding journey. Against all odds, they have grown and celebrated their differences and challenges. In times when competitive race, egos and mistrust bring down even the best of equations, this extraordinary pair has set an example of inspiration and encouragement for the rising entrepreneurs in the country.

"Your sibling is someone you can trust with your lives, even in the worst of circumstances; they bring out the best in you!" Abhishek shares a well-meaning look at his sister who he has partnered as a brother, a friend and a guide through this exciting journey of Kreate Konnect. Despite the difference in their age, habits, lifestyles or interests, it is their mutual respect and a welcoming attitude towards their opinions and perspective that has allowed to duo to continue persistently with a symbiotic growth at both personal and professional levels. It is indeed a joy to witness such a partnership that helps to restore belief and security in the precarious world of enterprises. Whether it was helping his little sister get away from trouble at home as a kid, or encouraging this blossomed adult to explore her career path, Abhishek has proven his worth as a loyal and supportive brother. Arushi, on the other hand, with her eagerness to learn and participate, has always been a voice of reason and support that Abhishek can count on. It is this emotional connection and synergy that the both share, along with their own individual educational, experiential or intellectual merit that has brought them far and high on their journey of success, and the road surely appears to be getting only better from here!

To give your product the value and sale they deserve, visit www.kreatekonnect. com,LinkedIn:/company-beta/10182359, and Facebook: /kreatekonnect.

Manzil Events *was co-founded by siblings* **Supriya** *(left) and* **Anand** *(right) with a vision to provide one-stop solution for organizing corporate meets, exhibitions and other such events.*

The Ultimate Destination

Manzil Events *by Supriya & Anand*

When things are falling down below
And you know there is nowhere to go.
Turn around and look at me,
For you, my shoulders will always be.

Some words help one to get around in the world. While some words mean the world. There are few lucky people in this world you can proudly say that the words said to them (however rhetoric and poetic they may have sounded) have been actualized into reality. There are even fewer people who can smile and nod at you when you ask them whether they have such people in their lives who make such deep words come true. When you come across such people, though, know that you have stumbled into the little miracles of life and that there will inevitably be a beautiful history behind the people. Be sure to ask, to probe a little so that you may find a story worth telling. I say this because I come with experience; an experience that brought me to stumble upon such people who have brought new meanings to words, to inspiration and to what it takes for equations to become bonds for lifetime.

Anand and Supriya have known each other a long time now. They may be as opposite as the poles but they get along just fine. They hold the same spirit of ambition, endearing attitude and the will to perfection close to heart. They have an uncanny resemblance when it comes to their love for fitness and more importantly, they share the same DNA. They are siblings by birth after all! Supriya, elder of the two, swears by the gym and believes in adventures as the true teachers of life. An avid wildlife enthusiast, she is also often found connecting with animals, reading up about them or petting the creatures she meets in her day to day life. With her educational qualification in the field of commerce, Supriya has been adding experiences around business management and corporate functionality to her cap of feathers. Anand, younger by two years, is a reservoir with the depth and calmness reflecting only as subtle smiles on his face. With the kind of maturity and insight he has attained at his age, Anand is perceived as an extremely level-headed person with a piercing will towards his goal. His acumen also reflects strongly in his love for adventure and he lives for the adrenaline kick that different forms of exciting activities bring to him. The entrepreneurial streak is what drives him with the same thrill in real life. In fact, he began his experiments with business ideas back when he was in the eighth standard. Even during his years of graduation, while he was pursuing his bachelor's degree in commerce, Anand was trying some or the other form of business venture, gaining first hand experiences of the nuances, tricks and treats of the world of enterprises.

It was during this stage that Anand stumbled upon the idea of events.

"I realized that event management did not require a lot of initial investment, could be managed lucratively even for an entry level person like me, and most importantly, this was something I knew I would enjoy incredibly," Anand speaks reflecting on the genesis of his new idea.

Thus, with a goal in mind, a destination of all event solutions in plan, Anand started his event management company in partnership with then friend and business associate Himanshu. This marked the beginning of Manzil Events as a one stop goal for anyone seeking successful event management.

"I was perfectly fascinated by the idea of Manzil (destination) and had already become a part of it as background support for my brother," Supriya shares, "having always appreciated his entrepreneurial attempts, I knew he was putting his heart and soul into it and I would do anything to make it work for him."

Having sustained even through their years of graduation with the business, the siblings and their partner decided to continue this as their mainstream enterprise after graduation thus giving Anand his full-fledged career a kick-start with his own venture. Supriya continued to work for a reputed name in the country while still providing back end support to her brother.

However, it all wasn't hunky dory in the Manzil Events camp as the momentum brought the company into mainstream channels. After the first six months of baby steps into growth, the venture started incurring heavy losses and started running downhill with some unexpected set-backs.

"We had conceptualized and produced a massive food festival, this was executed after more than eight months of aggressive planning and research, we were 100% sure and confident of this event turning into a mega success, which would fetch us a good brand name and the required profits to expand quickly," Anand recalls.

However, as true nature of life finds its reflections in the most unplanned and unexpected ways, so did it show its unforeseen turns this time for the Manzil team.

This was indeed a challenging time for the entrepreneurs who had been investing their heart and soul for the efforts and were evidently baffled with things going out of hand for them. It was also around this time that misfortune struck the enterprise and Himanshu, the managing partner of Manzil had to leave the business to relocate to his home town in Kolkata. However as devastating as this break in partnership was for Anand, it was equally tormenting for Surpiya to see her brother go through this phase despite his earnest efforts. For ordinary people, this would have been a heartbreaking situation. But for the siblings, this was a time for strengthening their will, after all, they are not what you would call average, ordinary people.

"During this stage of what we now call the 'fortunate crisis', a lot of discussions went on in the family about the next best steps to take. Our parents came out in strong support and encouragement which was an incredulous relief, especially for Anand," Supriya recalls. "It was around this time that during one such conversation, our father suggested that I ask my sister if she would like to officially join me as a partner in the enterprise. It took me a while to even register how I could have missed such an obvious choice! She had been with me through the crests and trough of Manzil, and knew the business inside out. I was certain that the partnership was going to be a hit, even before I asked her!" Anand speaks with obvious delight. Supriya, as someone who stands tall for support for her younger brother, agreed willfully. Thus began the entrepreneurial partnership of the brother and sister that has blossomed into bigger and better results that perhaps either could have imagined.

Bringing deeper and more diverse perspectives to the table, the siblings discussed the probable causes of the failures and successes and evaluated the key essentials of what would make Manzil really work. They brought into picture the critical focus of products and services that had earlier been missing in an attempt to try everything in their capacity. "Finally we chose to focus and develop just four verticals: Corp. events, Brand activations, Entertainment and Weddings, after studying our previous experiences and the current business trends. We kept in mind that we had to cover our basics first rather than only chase a wild dream," Anand explains with insight after having visibly adapted to the new strategic approach.

"In the past we had suffered, being badly hit financially and morally. Consequently, this deliberate reformation was a turning point when we decided to narrow our ambitions & there after followed a focused approach towards building the company."

But history is witness to the fact that no reformation happens without turmoil or pain. Fairly true was this phenomenon for the siblings as well. Many levels of changes were being witnessed in the internal processes as well as the external products of Manzil and this clearly showed its effects.

"Although it was a welcome relief to have Supriya onboard as a new partner, it would be a lie to say that the transition was a smooth one," Anand shares candidly. Having set his own way of working and placing a system into operation with Himanshu, Manzil had established a drift which had to be considerably altered once Supriya joined in. There were differences in decision making, in policies and even in the kind of expectations that the siblings had from each other.

"We had our share of clashes in the beginning. It could have been annoying at some level but I have to admit it really did help us to define our roles, ambitions and expectations more clearly than ever before," Supriya smilingly divulges. These clashes eventually turned into steps that helped them carve their individual roles in the enterprise and to set their own work mechanism that would consequently fit into each other's process – an achievement that is commendable considering how many partners in business have failed to accomplish despite years of experience and endeavour. This subsequent progress helped the siblings to develop and sustain an image and quality for Manzil that soon overcame the phase of failure and metamorphosed into a steady ship of successes. From extending the partnership to building a team, Surpiya and Anand now stand tall with a crew of twenty-two members, equally dedicated and oriented in their motivation and vision for the organization. Sitting in their office, watching the team float effortlessly from one task to another, intricately involved and yet efficiently independent, one gets the feel of a large organism thriving and growing with little functions pushing forth the force of life.

The force of life for the siblings too thrives forward centered around, but not limited to, the ethos of Manzil. As siblings first and partners consequently, both Anand and Supriya ensure that the delicate balance between work and home is balanced.

"I can't say that we have cracked the code for keeping the work and life equilibrium intact, but I am happy to say that it is one of priorities and both of us innately work towards holistic development rather than running a race where nothing really maybe won," Anand reflects with experiential wisdom. It is further an assertion of their personal equation which holds as the foundation of whatever the siblings have accomplished in their professional space. Some may find it surprising to an extent to watch the pair riffraff through their everyday affairs with the same passion and innocence as that of teenaged siblings who quarrel, quest, celebrate and cheer the presence of each other in their lives despite the drama.

"Far from being annoyed, I think we really cherish the difference and objectivity we bring in each other's life. Not only has this helped us form a reliable and compatible relationship at the work front but also fantastically helped our personal equation to evolve symbiotically," Supriya shares.

As the duo plans their future with Manzil, diversification, scaling up and backward integration are a few sentiments that appear visualized in their heads. The harmony with which the duo has developed and strengthened the venture is a very apparent reflection of how their harmonious growth has been even in their immediate environment.

"Our family is very liberal and supportive; they have always stood by us during our journey and passively helped us throughout. We have been brought up in an ecosystem where our parents always believed that children should be given the freedom to take major decisions, make mistakes, fall and learn to stand by on their own. This attitude was instrumental in making us confident and strong individuals." Sitting on a couch in his office, Varun shares this emotion, his eyes betraying the impact this personal element has on his life. And yet, sitting in that office, watching the team of Manzil go about creating, brainstorming, building and managing the most important moments in the lives of people, I can clearly see that the personal sentiment resonating as a wave of energy in the work place. The spirit that has risen from the bond of a family and especially in these siblings has brought not only their ambition out to a platform of creativity and entrepreneurial epitome, but also helped to create and sustain a work culture that is an aspiration as well a professional delight.

In a world which is so aggressively focused on competing and winning, Manzil and its team sets forth an example that believes in a more holistic ethos of creating an impact as a parameter of success. "Obviously there is a tense edge of competition in this industry. But we are not intimidated by it. We believe in building strong and long term relationships with our clients instead of simply bagging projects in numbers," Supriya has, in such simple words, bared more than mere approach to competition. In fact she has revealed this tremendous level of satisfaction that the siblings enjoy in their work by the simple comfort they feel towards the direction in which they are headed. This subtle and yet intense sentiment is what I would believe is responsible for bringing the world together through words. No matter what the scenario is, no matter how high or low the stage of life maybe, the attitude of this dynamic pair of siblings turned entrepreneurs is sufficient to restore the faith that one's words and actions are the truest and most valued support one can offer. And offered they have to one another – their unconditional support and faith in bringing this partnership to life and livelihood. One can see many elements in this equation that evoke your faith in the power of siblings. On the one hand, Supriya's willingness to support her brother through his times of need reflects her concern and love for her brother, on the other hand, Anand's invitation to his sister to partner up with her is a symbol of humility and faith that the siblings share without the clash of egos that could have come in between. While their entrepreneurial equation teaches them to respect each other's opinions and individuality, their personal equation has brought to them an understanding and patience that comes only when one is accepted and appreciated whole-heartedly. To have each other by their side, to connect professionally and in the principles of life in general has been a trait that Anand and Supriya inspire in many others to follow. While it may have been adversaries that brought them to the beginning of this partnership, it has been their own diligence and meticulous hard work that has brought it this far to its 'Manzil'.

For unmatched and hassle-free experience with managing events, contact www.manzilevents.com, Facebook: /ManzilEvents, Twitter: @manzilevents.

Onu *(left) and* **Oru** *(right), the sister duo started the apparel brand* **OnuOru** *to make available trendy fashion without compromising on comfort.*

The Fabrics of Sisterhood

OnuOru by Onu & Oru

The theories of the world say that path breakers and achievers come out of the ordinary because of their individual efforts, struggles, lessons from failures and more importantly, drive to accomplish skills they have built for themselves from scratch. Commonly, the individual is glorified for the summit they have reached and that is the end of it. However, a school of thought, more intensive in its research and observation explains that the success of a front-runner is the result of a lot of factors that may or may not have been the intended or controlled result of the showman's performance. A plethora of elements, like genetics, environment, financial backings, cultural ambience and immediate personal support system make a huge difference into making someone successful. It wouldn't be a far-fetched claim to make that it is actually the most critical people in your life that make the most significant contributions to helping your endeavours achieve the hallmark you can claim.

Who says you need to look out into the world to meet the diversity of people who can influence you? There are gems of talents within the same geography, institutions and surprisingly even within the same family. Particularly so when people you have known since childhood walk in as adults offering their support, you can tell that in the battle of succeeding in life, you have unmatchable strength in sheer company. Blessed with the company of each other, and an environment that inculcates and supports versatile and challenging interests in them, Onupreeta and Orunima, two young girls grew up to make a story of their own lives, one that reinforces one's strength in the institution of families and goes on to define how companionships transcend occasions or domains and can become the comrade-in-arm to walk up the ladder of success.

The sisters, although five years apart in age, have often been considered as twins in the way they are connected and compatible with each other. Cultivating the same interests in arts including the skills of painting, singing and dancing as children, they learned to appreciate creativity and inculcate the same holistic attitude in their characters, whether while dealing with professional dimensions or personal spheres. Growing up, they pursued their individual interests, both as hobbies and as professions in their individual lives. But it was a strange stroke of luck that brought them back together again, and this time in ways that connected them beyond being sisters.

While Onu grew up to pursue her degree in communication after a bachelor's degree in commerce, Oru graduated in arts and then moved to Abu Dhabi as started her professional career with the Gulf Air as an airhostess. The elder sibling, Onu established herself in the dynamic city of Mumbai and spent a decade dedicating herself to the world of advertising. For Oru, after a few years of flying, the professional switch came that brought her back to Mumbai where she began singing professionally, building on an interest she had nurtured growing up with her interest in music. In principle, the women have been more alike than different despite the seemingly varied choices and interests of their adult lives. However, moving and working in the same city during their individual journeys, somehow connected the sisters again that can be contributed for what unfolded eventually to change their professional equation drastically.

You know how sisters can sit together and pour their hearts out to each other? It is a natural process of both bonding collectively as well as growing individually. For Onu and Oru too, this was a process they indulged in very often, especially since Oru moved into the same city.

"It all happened on a particular Saturday afternoon when we were talking about what is going on in our lives. It was then that the conversation steered to our favorite topic of how we should do something on our own," Onu recalls.

Having worked for other people and directing their respective skills and experiences for external agents had brought the sisters enough confidence to know the tactics and mettle of what it takes to build something of their own. And the best part was that they knew they had it in them. "The idea of venturing into an enterprise for ourselves was definitely on the table for a while, it just erupted into a decision that day," Oru adds after her sister, in typical harmony that the two share.

"You can always expect the sisters to be echoing each other's opinions or even at a deeper level, each other's vibes!" a friend had fondly mentioned about the dynamic duo.

When the siblings narrowed down on creating their own apparel brand as their venture, it came as no surprise to the near and dear ones.

"As young girls, we had learned how to stitch, design, paint and sew our own clothes. This way, we could create something new to wear and give wings to our imagination all at once!" Oru explains. However, this creative instinct has not just been limited to the sisters for their personal designs.

"Oru has been designing her clothes for her shows for a while now. And she has always been acclaimed by people for the kind of genius designs she creates for the stage."

Onu is one to praise her sister but more importantly goes on to reveal how well processed the deliberation on starting an apparel brand has been as whimsical it appears on a superficial level.

Thus began the amazing journey of the brand OnuOru which launched in the month of August 2013. Explaining the beginning, Oru reveals, "We started right after freezing the idea and didn't wait too much for the thought to wither away. We immediately bought fabrics and started designing our range; that's how passionate the idea was for us."

Designing their first consignment, the duo came up with a unique style of sarees which became an instant hit! The sisters adhered to the well thought principles of a newly formed enterprise and kept their expenses to a minimum from the beginning.

"We started out with a basic page on Facebook to showcase our work and to reach out to people. This way, we were available for orders, could display our work in public and yet, be economical in our approach," Oru explains the dynamics.

Behind this seemingly spontaneous and emotive pair or sisters are hearts and minds that are determined, deep rooted and extremely hard working. A focused attitude reflects impressively as they explain their aggressive growth and steady plans and targets for the future.

"Having sold out our first range of apparels, we built a website and prepared ourselves with a variety of clothing lines for e-retailing. We are known for our play of colours and wearability. We make stylish clothes but not at the cost of comfort. This is our unique selling point. Our clothes capture the gypsy heart and so people like wearing them," Onu speaks proudly and knowingly. Having diversified from sarees to nomadic wear and recently into men's apparels, OnuOru has left no trace of doubt for anyone to believe that the sisters are not here to make their own space in the wild world of fashion.

Within three years of being operational, the siblings have managed to create their own identity through the uniqueness of their perspective on fashion wear. Their designs are bold, their fabrics stressing on comfort and their colors speak volumes about the imagination that the duo let loose when it comes down to pouring their creativity. While on a professional level it speaks for a clutter breaking collection that gives the sisters an edge over the commonplace brands of fashion in the country, it takes you to another level of understanding of the mettle of the sisters who are bold, dynamic, think out of the box and do not hesitate in pouring their hearts into their work.

"Our designs are in a way expressions of ourselves and our passion. That is what art should be – honest expression that is meant to make people better, happier and more rejuvenated with the experience," Onu adds with a glint of wisdom in her ideas.

The Alchemist theory explains that if you want something badly enough in the world, the entire cosmos comes together to help you achieve it. The same applies legitimately for Onu and Oru as well. Not only have they been endowed with creative and adventurous streaks – assets that come very handy in the world of enterprises, but their environment and people around them have also played a major role in making circumstances favorable for their pursuit of accomplishment. Behind the success of these dynamic women are two very strong and patient men who have established their support and faith in the sisters as their backend sustenance. "Our spouses have been one of the major reasons behind us who have helped us to come this far in our venture," Onu speaks for herself and on the behalf of her sister too.

"Even without being directly involved in their enterprise, the respective husbands have been helping out with understanding and accommodating sustenance."

It is not uncommon to hear that working women have had to give up on their professional career under the burdens of responsibilities of the domestic sphere. Especially so for women with their own business with stretching boundaries and unearthly timings, the challenge has been overwhelming to balance between work and home; many have succumbed to the pressure and given up their dreams. In the light of this challenge that holds many women back from realizing their dreams, the nuptial support that backs Onu and Oru is a refreshing relief. "Not only do we feel content on that front, knowing that our husbands have our back, but we also receive great encouragement to push our own boundaries and explore higher roads each time. That is the kind of support every woman yearns for in her life for her professional growth," Oru echoes the siblings' sentiment with no uncertain gravity. From financial backing to looking after the family to emotional support, the sisters have found the strength in their own family which has helped them cross the bridge.

"Even our parents have been a delightful agent of strength. From childhood, they have inspired us to find our own roads and build our own wings to fly. They have never doubted our caliber and always been full of words to encourage us forward," the sisters agree in overwhelmed harmony. It would be both fair and necessary to acclaim the little universe that the sisters have created and been blessed with in their lives that has brought them to their pedestal today.

With great achievements come even greater lessons just as with great climbs appear greater stumbles through the hurdle. If you bring up a conversation about the challenges that OnuOru has encountered through their journey, you will be surprised with an unexpected excitement and patience with which they talk about the difficult times as their best friends in retrospect. "We started fresh with a lot of impulsive decisions and excitement. We could have gone either way from there – up or down. But it was our challenges that opened our eyes, sharpened our wit and inspired us to set our holding deeper in the ground. It is possible that we would have soared unthinkingly had our limitations not compelled us have a wider foresight and diligent attention to minor details." Onu can blow your mind away with an insightful revelation and go back to a naughty giggle that will leave you stunned.

One of the most difficult decisions and its aftermath for the sisters was to unearth the established constructions of their respective careers and give up the comforts of stabilized income and certainty.

"It was a definite risk, for both of us to quit and start from ground zero, there's no denying that. Even though we jumped into making this decision with a hundred percent involvement, we were very aware of the stakes," Oru shares while Onu adds vehemently, "This was clearly one of the toughest decisions of my life to make. But I am glad I did!" Boot strapping with their own savings to push the venture, the sisters have been through their phase of financial struggle but always had each other's back through the telling times.

"We keep the expenditure to a minimum and work with a small team of artisans. We believe in hard work with dedication and that has been enough to bring us this far," Oru speaks with humility. Not that getting up one fine day and setting up an enterprise has been a cake walk for them, as the sisters have had to search and rigorously for everything from fabrics to equipment, delivery channels to financial management. Splitting responsibilities between the two, their's has been a profile management based on skills and experiences that each has experienced over the years. Onu brings her extensive experience of working with some of the most famous brands of the country to contribute to the marketing side of the business, her association with start-ups helping immensely with the strategic decisions for business development. Oru, on the other hand, brings the zing of her exposure with a diversity of culture, style and fashion after having travelled extensively for her work as an airhostess as well as a singer. Her keen sense of observation and taste for creative designing helps OnuOru delve into their out of the box fashion.

As siblings and entrepreneurial partners, the duo has come a long way in life. From travelling for work across different geographies, to creative wrestling over new designs and patterns to work on, the sisters have shared experiences through work or home that have changed them as both indiduals as well as partners. Despite the challenges, differences and unpredictability, or much rather, especially because of it, they have been able to assess their own limitations and strengths. Not only has this resulted in building an enterprise that has helped them both express their dreams and create ownership of something that is making its appreciated mark in the world, but has also opened up a new dimension of their equation with one another.

"To live, fight, learn and celebrate with your sister as your best friend is something we have done growing up and living in proximity for a big part of our lives. But to partner up in an enterprise has brought us to an even deeper understanding of one another and taught us to respect each other's differences and opinions as our own," the sisters reflect in consensus. It may not be far removed from reality to say that the sisters have found the mantra to what makes an equation between two siblings work. No matter what this fabulous pair does in life, they admit they would want to do it together. Perhaps, the thread of this relation is what helps them stitching their success into its rightful place and provide a fabric for the world to see and learn from!

To grab amazing deals on fashion wear for men and women, visit www.onuoru.com, or their Facebook, Twitter and Instagram pages @onuoru.

Rajat *(left)* and **Abhishek** *(right) thought of* **Poolmyride** *to solve the daily commute problem by enabling easy private vehicle carpooling, thereby also ensuring support to the environment.*

Riding through the ad-Venture

Poolmyride by Rajat & Abhishek

They sit on a funky couch punching away on their computers like there is no tomorrow. There is a constant exchange of technical details among them, in words that might sound alien to a person with a non-technical background and yet, there is a warm and comfortable feeling around this space that is called their office. The two engineers in picture could pass off as ordinary men of ordinary faculty in the first glimpse. But unlike most ordinary lives, theirs speaks of a story that has gone beyond basic engineering, beyond 'work' and beyond two people sitting on a couch speaking technical mumbo-jumbo. How can you tell? Take a peek at their screens – it betrays their passion, dipped in ingenuity and purpose. While their background information on the internet would reveal association with big brands, work experience that make them good hires across multinational recruitments, it is really their mettle to break away and build something of their own – something meaningful, productive and instigating consciousness, that attracts the most attention.

Till a few years ago, Rajat Talwar was a full-time employee in Bangalore, working for one of the most reputed names in the world. Also working with him was his loving wife in the same organization. A typical day for Rajat included crossing the bustling roads of Bangalore, taking a metro ride to work and immersing himself in software development.

As Rajat shares, "We walked to our office in Bangalore, as we stayed a five-minute walking distance away from Amazon. I actually realized during this time that how much time gets wasted, as I used to spend three hours travelling to work and back in Delhi. We saved time by walking to work here, and the saved travel time became time for building up Poolmyride after Abhishek suggested it."

A fitness freak, Rajat likes maintaining a healthy regime and prefers a walk to work any day over sitting behind the wheel. His passion, apart from developing better engineering platforms, also includes exploring new elements in life, learning new skills and teaching them too. However stable and content that sounds, a phone call from someone who he shares a past led to a chain of events and ultimately changed the way the world around him would shape up.

Abhishek had a different cycle of life going on around him not more than five years ago. A successful android developer, he enjoys programming, body building, adventures and spending time with friends. What he never enjoyed, however, was driving about twenty-two kilometers to work in the National Capital Region of the country, stuck in jams, in the frenzy of horns, pollution and unending queues of cars with empty backseats. "There has to be a way to end this," he would often catch himself thinking.

And a way he did think. Not only did he think but also worked on it, day and night, in-between work hours, on weekends and vacations. Because his idea not only had him driving forward out of passion, but also got him to build an idea for a start-up, which would eventually surface in the Indian market as a solution to one of the most critical urban problems that the country is facing. And this is what brought Rajat and Abhishek, brothers by birth, friends for life, together in a way that changed their lives. As software developers, the brothers have been building solution applications for different people and reasons. So this doesn't come as a surprise that they should build an application for themselves with such ingenuity and utility.

"I would be bugged being stuck in traffic everyday commuting to and fro from work. The gravity of today's traffic and pollution situation in the country is not a mystery anymore and we had often talked about it. And then one day, instead of simply cribbing about the situation, I decided to become a part of the solution and do what we do best – build an application, which in its own unique way would help to curb down both the problem with one strike!" explains Abhishek.

Thus, was born one of the most unique applications of the country that connected technology with the need of the people.

Poolmyride is a ride sharing application. It is a carpooling app that allows you to connect with people in real-time to share/ seek a ride or offer a ride while traveling on the same route. The USP? This app claims to be the most intelligent app among all the carpooling apps on Store mainly because it has been built an excellent geo-fencing feature that alerts a user when a carpool is made near him/ her. The actual journey of Poolmyride left the screen of Abhishek's laptop and started building into reality the day the software was ready, when he instinctively turned to his brother – his best critic and friend, to explain his idea of quitting his job and dedicating himself fulltime to Poolmyride.

"I was ecstatic to hear his idea and application. I wanted to pitch in and make the iOS application too because that's what I had been doing professionally in my previous two jobs. And thus, our story began," Rajat exclaims. Contrary to appearance, it wasn't a spur of the moment decision for the siblings because it was in their hearts to explore something substantial and sustainable on their own and it was only rational that they would choose Poolmyride as their path ahead.

A lot of hurdles were passed by the sheer passion and determination that the duo had. Without an ounce of doubt in their venture, they were lucky enough to find mutual support.

"He is the one person I will trust my life with; there couldn't have been a better choice for partnership!" Abhishek admits. With the same principles, ideologies, interests and backgrounds, the connection between the tech-brothers goes beyond being business partnership and nonetheless acts as the best incentive. It is also the strength and understanding in this brotherhood that spills over in the family. Rajat's wife was not only excited and forthcoming in her encouragement for his venture but also supported it initially by continuing her job and eventually shifting to Poolmyride fulltime in solidarity.

Meant to be? He laughs with a slight jest but quickly turns serious and you can tell this means a lot more to him than a stroke of fate. There was the educational background that ignited his interest in development but, as he admits, it was also a lot of hard work, experience and self-tutoring that went into bringing him the expertise and confidence to make Poolmyride happen.

"When you have to run a company, you have to be the jack of all trades!" he winks jokingly, obviously having mastered many more levels of skills than being merely a jack. Abhishek, on the other hand has been fascinated with the creativity that technology can sprout from his own hands. "To be able to create a user experience which is both enjoyable as well as utility based is what gives me the kick," Abhishek declares. A much bigger fan of utility than merely want-based commercialism, Abhishek has poured his heart and soul not only into generating the idea but also making Poolmyride an experience that encourages people to adopt this problem solving medium with ease and comfort.

A question on the journey and experience, in contrast to working for other organizations will spring almost the same answers from the duo, who in true sense, seems to resonate the same passion and contentment like the nature of two branches of the same tree. Not only do they declare this as a venture full of excitement and satisfaction but also admit to the perks of working for themselves as "fulfilling – that's the word I would use for Poolmyride. This is not to say that whatever had to be achieved has been done, but to work for your ideology and to do it with someone who understands your sentiments behind it and respects the ideology it was built on – that is the biggest incentive," Abhishek adds ardently.

They say that joys and hurdles halve themselves when you have someone to watch your back, the Talwar brothers are a live example of this fact. "I am not saying that it has been an easy ride. But little things can iron out when you know you have the big brother watching, if you know what I mean," Abhishek jokes with a wink.

When it comes to traditional families, these first cousins have an ideal set of parents – with their simple concerns, experienced advice and warnings of what the future might await. Needless to say, both sets of parents were not instantly excited about having their sons gamble on an idea that they, quite frankly, couldn't even see an office for! "We were working from home, for crying out loud! I understood their apprehensions of not having the stability of a salaried income and of having to quit such a reputed and lucrative job," Rajat reflects on his parents' reaction, "but the best part was that Abhishek and I believed in each other and that's what eventually got mom and dad to offer their blessings too."

Although this meant a lot of expectation on their shoulders, the brothers endured it without intimidation and even worked on freelance projects to keep the money flowing, to give them the cushion they might eventually need. Although having secured funds with the help of an accelerator, the brothers still take their financial steps cautiously enough to stabilize their expenditures. What adds to the trouble is that Poolmyride does not have a concrete revenue model.

"We tried a model in the initial phase but that did not work out well – this was probably our first failure. So we are still working on that front," Rajat explains, only to be complimented swiftly by his brother's optimistic opportunism.

"This really gives us the chance to focus entirely on our application development to make sure that it grabs the customer attention at the right nerve. We are confident that once our product is rock solid, it will only be a matter of time before the revenue generation kicks in the right order." Although admitting this to be easier said than done, the brothers are excited about the latest developments they have made from past experience and market research – factors that help an organic growth of Poolmyride to maintain a top slot in the competitive market.

Speaking of growth, what is it that keeps the boundaries from spilling over between the personal and professional fronts for the duo is an interesting take away in itself. "We're software developers first and co-founders only second. Hence dedication to the product development comes as our first priority," explains Abhishek in all seriousness.

However, as the specific role definitions and skills have chiseled for the duo, their work diocese has also seen expansion and demarcations with time. With the team expanding as Poolmyride finds a stoic foothold in the market, while Abhishek has fixed his concentration on the android team, Rajat heads the iOS section of development. However, this compartmentalization does not limit the brother's involvement in each other's verticals.

"We both have the same vision and intention; it is also true that we can both handle each other's criticism and advice with absolute objectivity and maturity – I think it has to do with us sharing the same DNA," Rajat admits with a glint of a smile that reflects with a stark similarity in both the brothers. With this simple and effective equation, the clash of interests is difficult to arise. However, it would be naïve to say that there are none. "We have had our share of opinions that sometimes don't overlap, pretty much like the conflicts we have with each other even as children. But I guess that's what sibling do they bring out different sides of the world on the same plate and then the best options are debated and eventually picked!" Abhishek enunciates with a deliberation that has come with what seems like years of debating and picking with his older brother.

You can see the delight in the eyes of Rajat and Abhishek as they begin their day with their team, brain-storming over ideas, taking feedback or simply being engrossed in their computer screens. In-between the intense moments of work and discussions, explorations and achievements are also the lighter moments that the brothers share with each other and the team.

"When I am taking a break, if I come across something that I know Rajat will like for a fact, I just share with him on the internet. You are sure to hear a sudden crack of laughter from another end of the room after sometime and you can tell he has just checked his chat box," Abhishek jests. Knowing the mantra that makes the other click or tick, the brothers have worked around their own attitude, skill and work approach to accommodate each other's opinions and space. With accomplishments coming to them in form of recognition, support and user response, the Talwar brothers clearly know they are on the right track, especially when they have each other to deliberate and depend on, a luxury that sure does not go unnoticed in a cut-throat world of enterprises where trust and compatibility are a bigger challenge than an enterprising idea that would or would not work.

Having said that, it is not difficult to observe the humility with which the Talwars have definitely determined heads on their shoulders. If you try congratulating them on their success, you will see a sense of gratitude and humility ooze not only in their words but also their attitude. While Rajat clearly admits that their bench mark for success needs for them to work a lot harder and climb a lot higher than their current status, Abhishek extends his opinion about success to be a lot more than the revenue generated and users acquired.

"There's a lot more to be done with Poolmyride," he explains. "In terms of technology, services and also opportunity that makes people not only want to use the application but also know that this is not just a swanky facility but the need of the hour. When that happens, I will know that we have succeeded in the mission that we set out to achieve."

The brothers will not boast about their accomplishments unless really poked. Neither will they show off the various media coverage, mentions and acknowledgement they have received since the kick-start. A proud mention comes into conversation about their recognition at the internationally acclaimed platform of Carma Accelerator in Ireland at an early stage of the establishment of Poolmyride that not only brought them the encouragement the young entrepreneurs needed at that stage but put them at par on a stage where they got the opportunity to interact and connect with some of the stalwarts of the world of entrepreneurship. With confidence in their eyes, motivation in their hearts and each other's undying support at their side, Rajat and Abhishek have come a long way from a simple idea that generated during a traffic jam. More than anything else, it has been the bond that the brothers have come to cherish even stronger and deeper than before. Having seen each other through the best and the worst of times, it is this partnership that has brought them to appreciate and respect each other against all odds and that perhaps, has been the mantra for turning their venture into an adventure that the brothers have been sailing on with pride, confidence and sorority.

Go ahead, pool your ride! Visit www. poolmyride.com, Facebook: /poolmyride, Instagram: poolmyride2.0, Twitter: @poolmyride.

Purplehed *is the creation of brother duo* **Ashutosh** *(left) and* **Anurag** *(right) which aims to produce art that has a global appeal – music that soothes and dance that inspires.*

A Story of Hearts and Beats

Purplehed *by Ashutosh & Anurag*

If music was the heartbeat, and dance the body, if music was the wick and dance its flame, and if music were an essence and dance the breeze that transmits its perfume into far off lands, one would feel that each is necessary for the existence of the other, that both complement and enhance each other and fit into one another like a jigsaw puzzle. When this expression comes alive, in whichever form possible, it brings about results that have a deep impact on the lives that make it as well as witness it. What it takes to build this impact is unpredictable; sometimes a natural gift or twist of fate, sometimes transformational journeys and sometimes, just inherent dreams waiting to sprout into reality. And sometimes, it is a scheme of all these agents combined that brews an answer. Such is the turn of events in the lives of two men who though seemingly regular in their impressions, turned their lives around into becoming the reality that had perhaps been dreamed at least a generation before them.

Two engineers in different parts of the country were busy pursuing their education and their careers in the most traditional fashion. They began with promising careers, nurtured, harnessed through series of hard work that almost every youth in this country has to strive through to battle the fierce competition. They both also nurtured parallel interests – hobbies as most would call them. But what connected these two men was the drive to blossom these interests into concrete expressions – even professions as convention would designate. What also connected them was the madness to make their dreams come true despite the odds. And as fate would have it, what connected them was the same passion running through their veins into their hearts from the same father, with his passion and life dedicated to music. There was a dream – a dream to sprout his unrealized dreams into reality, to make a father proud and to dare life with their passion.

Ashutosh Upadhyay could pass off as a typical engineer, with his love for technology, a passion for creating new things and music plugged into his ears more often than not. But unlike most people who would fall into the conventional mold of a professional cycle, Ashutosh had a different calling that he paid attention to. His young heart called out to him with the melody of music and he answered. Although his vocational orientation was conventionally technical, his pursuit for music took him to experiment and experience different musical instruments. His exploratory spirit took him across countries to witness different cultures, styles of music and ultimately, to embrace his own ambition to conceive his unique style of music.

His sibling, Anurag Upadhyay found expression in another form and discovered the art of dance as his ignition for expression. After the pursuit of his degree in civil engineering, Anurag secured a conventionally reputed position in a well renowned organization of the country and continued his love for contemporary dance as a weekend hobby. He also completed a dedicated and difficult journey of three years to attain various certificates and diplomas in modern and contemporary dance forms. As romantic as the idea sounds, it wasn't a cakewalk for him either.

"I would bicycle my way through to these classes because I had to save money commuting. No matter what the traffic or weather was like, I was dedicated to making it to every single class," he reflects with a sense of pride.

Although the two led their individual lives of seemingly stable careers in their own individual worlds, a part of their hearts was always stuck around their passion for the art that they call and believe to be their first love. It was perhaps also that part of their heart that reached out to each other, as lovers of art, as friends and as brothers, with the same blood and spirit connecting them together. A transformation was long due on the cards and it would take what they fondly remember as 'the night that changed their fate' to bring new opportunities into the life of the siblings.

"It began with one of those regular conversations that we have as brothers, speaking our hearts out," recollects Ashutosh, "but despite the fact that Anurag was doing well in his career, I could sense the mental vacuum he felt in his life and I knew I had to nudge him to explore the roads he has been eagerly eyeing."

With thought provoking questions and encouraging words, Ashutosh finally got through to the voice that had been calling Anurag to pursue his love for dancing as a full time vocation.

"He didn't point out the risks involved, not for once did he mention the odds of this turning out to be a mistake I might regret. Instead, Ashutosh simply asked me if I wanted to do this, and then promised his unconditional support," reveals Anurag with honest gratitude. It is this sense of uninhibited backing that prompted Anurag to take his first steps towards learning and experimenting with contemporary dance form. It was also this respect for mutual aspirations, unending support and supreme confidence in one another that got the two brothers to combine their seemingly separate life paths and come together to design a venture that became an amalgamation between art and science, passion and profession. With this passion in their hearts, the duo formed Purplehed – a venture that became their platform to conceive and produce their expression with various genres of music and dance. Purplehed, which officially formulated in 2014, aspired to send out a message to its audience which would inspire them to dream and to break boundaries to realize those dreams. With Ashutosh and Anurag – brothers by birth and partners by choice, pouring their hearts into this venture, Purplehed became a symbol of music and dance, expression and enterprise, global and Indian. Purple – the colour of royalty, nobility, luxury, also denotes strength dignity, grandeur, devotion, peace, pride, mystery, independence, and magic. Headphones allow listening to music without disturbing others; hence Purplehed became a eulogy for the powerful expression of the self, of inspiration without hindrance and limitation of the outside world. The unique aim of this venture continues to create a unique connection of music and dance with people with an aim to explore their own creativity, to be inspired to break boundaries, to recreate Indian music in a form that is appealing in its modern texture and to bring it to a global audience. A message reaching to all the people that they are capable of living the way they want to – that all expressions are possible and viable and one need not be confined to conventions only because of the fear of no way out.

Thus, with the dream, a liberating message and a record label for music videos, the brothers launched Purplehed, with their first single release coming out in 2015. While their individual journeys had taught them perseverance, sincerity and helped them enhance the skills of their interest, it was the experience of working together that really showed them the real depth of their relationship. It is one thing to run a family business or for relatives to partner up in pursuit of an enterprise. But the brothers have a different connection. Not only do their skill sets align and their principles point in the same direction, but both Anurag and Ashutosh feel the same passion and understand each other's dedication that the outside world may label as madness.

Without a silver spoon or cushion of a business push to their advantage, the brothers have had to earn every skill and opportunity and turn odds into their favor. Working day jobs and finding time at night or over the weekends to polish their art skills has only made them stronger and more determined in their pursuit, a scenario that would have exhausted most in the crowd. While this journey was a slow and difficult one, it also helped the two men find firmer feet on the ground since everything they did, was built from ground zero, by their own hands and mind. The competitive perfectionism that runs in the family inspired this duo to stop at nothing but the best. The result is that two self-made men who have broken boundaries and followed their passions with each other's support have become examples of success. Collecting a ginormous buffet of skills through education, experience, work, internships, assistance and above all, dedication of moving beyond personal boundaries to make Purplehed work has brought the brothers to chisel their own skills. From music composition and choreography, which is their individual key expertise, the enterprising siblings have further enhanced their skills in production and film-making and further also self-constructed their abilities in organization management, business development, marketing and PR skills – all key ingredients that have come together to help not only the survival of Purplehed against fierce competition, but also internal and external operational challenges and the battle of inexperience against instincts.

But more than the skills and experience on their resume, it has been the key lessons of life and livelihood they have learned together that has brought them to a new spectrum of mutual respect and understanding of each other's strengths and weaknesses. A sibling is your biggest critic, your best friend, a competitor at best and a snitch who knows you inside out at worst, someone who has fought with you, laughed and cried with you and practically grown up with you, looking at all your strengths and weaknesses.

"To start from ground zero in your professional venture with your brother is as good as growing up from being a toddler to running the race holding each other's fingers – that is what it means for me to work with Ashutosh," expresses Anurag candidly.

The challenges from internal battles to external encounters have been in plenty for the duo. The biggest, in their admission, has been about building a consistent and reliable team from ground zero. Illustrating on a few challenges, that on hindsight, taught them a lot was a product they were working on which needed a back-up drive. But since the producer (Ashutosh) was travelling for work, it took him longer than anticipated to arrange for a back-up drive, during the course of which, the original drive crashed, causing a lot of damage in terms of money, time and deadlines that eventually led to a big failure in the name of Purplehed and caused a major morale crash for the team. What is their take away from this catastrophe?

"We came together as a team like never before, making efforts twice as hard, pushing ourselves without limits and eventually making up for all that loss we had suffered," Ashutosh declares with strength and experience, simply revealing how the brothers have acquired more strength and stability in their choices for the future than meets the eye and will stop at nothing to follow their dreams. With an array of products, especially four singles so far, Purplehed is nowhere falling short of proofs of its climb on the road to success. An album with twelve songs – titled Pipe Dreams – is due for release in 2018.

However independent it sounds in nature, the founders of Purplehed actually base their accreditation on the contributions, understanding and encouragement that their family has exchanged, enhanced and encouraged over the years. Whether it was related to expressing the desire to break away from the clutter and convention of predictable jobs to discover their own interest or simply to choose a path that may not even necessarily lead to a stable career, the brothers as well as their parents supported each other emotionally, financially as well rationally in the process of forming Purplehed, first as an idea and then as a venture. While the brothers have each other's back, it is also the consistent parental guidance, especially from their father that has helped them in creative and entrepreneurial guidance through this journey.

It has perhaps been the amalgamation of their passion and creativity along with their experience and enterprising spirit that has gotten the dynamic duo to find creative as well as financial sustainability. Having funded their initial phase through their own savings, the brothers have now managed to build a sustainable model through monetization, ads, product placements, music royalty/sales, and live performances. It is the zen within that perhaps the duo to find an external balance in their venture. Striking a balance between their personal and professional scales, the men find recreation in their passion and work in their interest. This is very simple. Both of us understand each other's strengths and weaknesses. We support each other and with mutual understanding we try to adapt as per the situation. So when it comes to the music department Ashutosh leads it and Anurag provides creative feedback throughout the iterative process. And when it comes to video production Anurag leads the thread in Direction, Editing, VFX, Motion Graphics, Complete film making and video production, while Ashutosh contributes all his creative feedback.

"Whatever is concluded best for the company we opt for. And the same approach is performed for all the other departments where both of us lead and take the final decision," Anurag describes an effortless symphony that gets the brothers working in compatibility and yet maintaining their own independent streak of thoughts and actions at Purplehed.

You can witness a clearheaded brain-storming session at Purplehed and know that the entire energy of the place is in sync. With the two brothers pouring in ideas ranging from creatives to strategy, finance to marketing, the entire team becomes a fountain of deliberations where all opinions are listened to and all contributions respected. "What most people forget as they rise higher up the ladder of success is that the key is to be a good listener," explains Ashutosh with the experience flooding in the undertone. "Anurag and I listen to each other a lot more than trying to shove our opinions down the other's throat. I guess, this is what our team watches and follows too!"

While mistakes have humbled and alerted the Upadhyay brothers, the achievements have given them the provocation and reward they deserve. Their success in the four releases and especially in their music video with a tribute to the Late Dr A.P.J. Abdul Kalam has left the youth inspired and deeply touched. But with their eyes held up to the sky and feet strong on the ground, you can tell that more than fame or success, it is the butterfly effect that each piece of art that Ashutosh and Anurag create that really stands out as their mark of success.

"If we have touched lives, if we have inspired people and especially youngsters to break the shackles of their boundaries and rise up to their full potential, as royally and strongly as Purplehed, our job is done."

With words of wisdom, the elder brother smiles and nods to indicate the end of the conversation and walks back to his team. You can tell that the air here breathes of music, of passion and of life; where the enterprise and its ethos really is a way of life instead of merely a career choice for the immaculate siblings. With sheer dedication, the brothers have risen from ground zero to building an ongoing movement in the shape of their enterprise, proving that when the roots are strong, the blossoms are bound to reach the world in true musical harmony.

 www.purplehed.com, Purplehed VEVO channel : www.youtube.com/PurplehedVEVO, Crunchbase: www.crunchbase.com/organization/purplehed, Facebook: /Purplehed, Instagram: /purplehed_ official, Twitter: @purplehedrecord, Soundcloud: / purplehed, Pinterest: /purplehed.

Creating designs that encapsulate a woman's very essence, **Quirksmith** *by* **Divya** *(left) and* **Pragya** *(right) promises the best in class craftsmanship in accessories to ensure bringing out the best of who you are.*

The Silvered Sisters

Quirksmith by Divya & Pragya

Opposites make it work, fitting in like a jigsaw puzzle. Where one falls, the other is the cushion. Where one is wood, the other is mellow, where one is creative, the other pragmatic. Any number of clichés in the world would be insufficient to reiterate the fact that it really is a compliment to be a complementary half of somebody else. What one really seeks in general existence is that which one lacks or aspires to become. Where one needs energy, one seeks coffee, where one needs flight, one seeks wings, where one needs sunshine, one seeks the day and when one needs support, one seeks a shoulder that one can lean on, unconditionally. The story of the two sides of a coin are incomplete without each other; more like the bigger purpose of their being the way they are remains unresolved unless they fit into the bigger machine of life. Philosophically, this streams into our consciousness as an idea that sounds both beautiful and fulfilling. But practically, having someone to complement you is a blessing that helps to iron out even the most absurd challenges that seem out of your league. It is no surprise then that our hands are made with perfect spaces to fit into a handshake; so that we may connect, communicate and collaborate with people who fill those gaps and bring out the best in us.

This is the story of one such pair of opposites that worked their magic together to show how perfectly complimentary contraries can be and that sometimes if life gives you people or moments contrary to yourself, you may just be receiving a blessing you are yet to unveil. Divya and Pragya had the fate of being born into the same family, a year apart from each other. By definition and birth, they are sisters from the same mother. By privilege, they have grown up together in the same environment, with the same upbringing, founding principles and circumstances to feed into their personality. But by choice and actions, they are beyond being just siblings. Despite the difference of a year, they are more like twins who became friends even before the roots of sisterhood sprouted in them.

"It was difficult to separate us as kids, we would always have each other's backs and fend for each other against everything else," Divya recollects fondly. However, if the two were met individually, it is hard to point what it is that brought the sisters together, considering how starkly different they are from each other. If one was sugar, the other pickle, if one was a lake, the other a waterfall, if one was the fruit, the other the roots. Divya, the elder of the two sisters, is known amongst friends and family as the chirpy one, a people's person and one with the creative crown wrapped around her head. Pragya, on the other hand, is conspicuous by her silence. She is the one who thinks, analyses and assesses every move. She is the one who holds the scepter of management out of the two. To the onlookers at a superficial level, these qualities set them apart from each other, making it impossible for them to be a part of the same fabric. But for those who have known Divya and Pragya would vouch for the efficiency with each they complement each other.

Apart from the obvious personality differences, the choices and interests in life have also varied for the siblings. While Divya has chosen jewellery designing as her education and vocation, Pragya has pursued the more technical dimensions of engineering for her degrees at the graduation and post-graduation level. Consequently, the former went on to handle a design studio as a part of her job, exploring the creative aspects of designing while the latter pursued her career after completing her Master's in Business Administration. The sisters were separated physically in the quest of their own careers. While Divya was in Mumbai with her studio work, Pragya was based out of Bangalore. This seemingly separate paths that the sisters had begun on played its own part in conjoining them in ways that most siblings don't dream or dare to explore.

"We always knew that we had to do something together. While half of it was based on our individual entrepreneurial streak, the other half was stemmed out of the fact that we are a close-knit duo that likes to do things together," Pragya builds on the connection that became their future endeavour. It was this streak and spirit, accompanied by the right set of opportunities that got the siblings to think about a venture into jewellery designing.

"I had so many ideas and plans in my head but I was a little apprehensive about implementing them. But I knew someone who had the right acumen to bring my ideas to reality; that was my sister!" Divya exclaims.

Thus, with an aspiration to bring their imagination and skills to use, the sisters started their own brand of silver jewellery collection by the name of Quirksmith in September 2014.

To unsuspecting simpletons, jewellery design in this story seems like the feat of the elder sibling who could and would single handedly be able to handle Quirksmith. However, for anyone who has delved into the realms of entrepreneurial journeys or even closely known people who have battled through it would tell you that the creation of the product is only the first half of the journey. The other half is the selling and pitching of the product that needs the combatting. Both Pragya and Divya knew how much they would need and complement each other on this journey they had embarked. "Divya is brilliant with her designs. She has over twelve years of experience to her credit and a creative head that can make magic out of mud!" Pragya compliments with absolute admiration.

However, as someone with complete awarenss of her strengths and weaknesses, the designer comes back with her share of input on the partnership. "If I were set sail in the sea of numbers and marketing strategies, I wouldn't know the mast from the mainsail! Pragya is the captain of my ship who helps me bring my creativity to the table for the customers."

It is beyond evident that the sisters not only complement each other in the different aspects of their entrepreneurial roles but are also very mindful and appreciative of these contributions.

Efficiently based on their skill sets and interests, the duo has divided their responsibilities within the venture. While Divya takes care of the design and product side, Pragya chairs the management and finance side of the business. Not only does this equation work smoothly for them but also gives them the opportunity to excel in their respective domains. Quirksmith has evolved over the years from being a weekend exploration for the sisters to becoming a full-time passion and investment.

"Back in the beginning, we had our individual work and commitments to deal with and hence we would devote our spare time and late nights into Quirksmith. But with time, our baby venture has evolved and so have we!" Pragya explains.

While for the first two years, it was possible for the duo to manage their enterprise while juggling through their own work, since the beginning of 2016, the dynamics of the venture began to change as the traction for Quirksmith increased and clientele started expanding aggressively. It was then that Pragya decided to quit her job and turn to the business fulltime.

"It was a really big decision and honestly, I was nervous about Pragya taking this step," Divya expresses being mindful of the financial obligations that both the sisters hold for their own families.

"But Pragya's belief in this move was a strong one. She was not only confident about the decision but also organized in her thoughts about the 'whats' and 'hows' that I could not have even imagined!"

Since June 2016, Quirksmith has become a full time occupation and passion for Pragya, while Divya rationally continues her commitment to the studio work along with squeezing every possible moment in her days and nights for Quirksmith. It is not without the compromises and understanding at a personal level for both the sisters that this feat has been achieved. With their respective spouses to support them and encourage them through thick and thin, both Pragya and Divya have formed a seamless equation of balance between work and home.

"To say that personal life and professional life doesn't spill into one another would be a naïve claim to make," Pragya reveals, "I can speak for the both of us that Quirksmith is not just 'work' for us but a matter of passion and dedication. And in this, there are no boundaries of where, when and how we accomplish our aim."

However, it has been challenging for the two to make it past some of the most critical boulders that life has tossed at them. For the lack of any initial funding, the duo had to boot strap their way through the first phase of investment. It took away appreciable chunks of their savings and put them in a high-risk position.

"Those were the days that mark the most difficult part of the enterprise. We had very limited resources, we could afford very limited channels of marketing and publicity and had to do with a constrained work force," Pragya recollects. But these sisters were not taught to back down in the face of challenges. Optimists to the core, the duo stormed their way to make the best of even their limitations.

"Honestly, I was amazed at the way we had learned to push our boundaries. That was a time that taught us to be respectful of our resources and to come up with the most innovative products and strategies during the hard times," Divya reveals in retrospect of her struggle. During this journey, they were advised and even assisted by their spouses who took out time from their own respective schedules to help with liasoning, strategizing and providing feedback wherever necessary. It has been a well-coordinated act of well-meaning people that has brought Quirksmith to its current state of accomplishment.

What started with the sisters showcasing the collection in flea-markets eventually evolved into being sought by the women who loved their jewellery collection. It was a mix of word of mouth, effective presence and a lot of running around to make visibility on different platforms that made Quirksmith eventually noticeable. Soon, they were being actively hunted for their unique and bold creations in silver. While it first started with a simple page on social media, today, Quirksmith is widely known across the internet and among its customers because of a range of patrons who instantly fell in love with the collections.

"You know, it is fair to say that categorical marketing strategies, meeting the right people and pitching the trendy designs has helped Quirksmith come to this stage of accomplishment and popularity but I know the deeper meaning that has brought all of this together." Pragya cracks the mystery by crediting it to the ethos that runs Quirksmith.

"It has always been our principle to make a product out of love and consideration. Whether this pertains to the dedicated and incredible talented artists of Rajasthan who help to melt the metal into gorgeous pieces of jewellery or the loving women who share their experience of these adornments, the biggest mark of success is how we have made people feel."

A rare quality in the world of enterprises where cut-throat competition and aggressive commercialism breeds over any sensitivity, humility is what radiates as the first impression when you speak to the sisters about the label of 'success'. With the true spirit of jewelling their lives with the beautiful smiles they have been bringing on the faces of women across the panel, Divya and Pragya feel accomplished in this phenomenon more than any numbers of figures that their enterprise has none-the-less climbed to achieved. "It is a spill-over effect, I think!" Divya jokes, "We set targets for ourselves but work generously towards strengthening the core of Quirksmith. It is no surprise then, with all the well-meaning hard work, we are able to achieve our targets at an astounding pace!"

Sitting in the ambience that makes Quirksmith, with the depth of Pragya's perceptiveness and the vibe of Divya's creativity, you cannot mistake this acknowledgement of success as even close to being arrogant. It is the confidence, belief and support that the sisters share that helps them in holding complete faith that the duo has used to convert their dream into reality.

"Even in the most trying times, I know my sister is here for me. She uplifts me in every sense possible and gives our personal relationship a whole new dimension too!" Divya resonates what is evidently the sentiment that the sisters share mutually. No matter what their individual diocese for the business front is, they add value and versatility to each other's life and livelihood! "We never forget how lucky we have been in life! First of all, it was always our dream to do something of our own. Secondly, the fact that we have each other to be able to realize this dream together is both a relief and a privilege," Pragya reflects. As a passing note, curiosity might get you to question them if they have any regrets. But you would no longer be surprised to see that well-meaning smile that the sisters exchange. You do not even need to hear them say 'no' in reply because it is more than obvious they have found what they had been seeking. If not Quirksmith, if not this life, the sisters would have built something else, led some other life, still accompanying each other, accomplishing new heights in whatever they would venture into, not only because they make an incredible pack of talent and perfection but extraordinarily because they have each other to prove to the world what the power of such an equation can create – whether it is jewellery, happiness, or even on the bigger canvas of life.

It is hard to tell what roads one takes in life, what choices are made and what stories are churned out of these choices made. Sometimes consciously, sometimes birth turns into a barrier and sometimes, into bonds that determine unimaginable fates of people. There are truths and tales waiting in front of each one of us, waiting to be knocked and explored. It is only fair then that the sisters, Divya and Pragya, so different in their fabrics but similar in their foundation should form the other ends of symmetry to complete the form. In creativity and strategy, in design and disposition, the duo makes the other complete in their attitude and skills. Not only do they complement each other's attributes but also inspire each other to strive to be better; not only in their enterprise but also in their personal hemispheres. Through struggles and satisfactions, through dips and developments, as individuals as well as in sync with one another, Divya and Pragya have shown the world that dreams, however improbable or natural they seem, work into reality with love, understanding and respect – a perfect symphony that the Quirksmith sisters have accomplished and inspire many others to follow suit.

Quirksmith

For accessories second to none in elegance and style, visit www.quirksmith. com, Instagram: /quirksmithjewelry, Facebook: /QuirkSmith.

Shemayel *(left) and* **Shurouck** *(right) are known as the* **Sugar Sisters** *after their startup that is well known for cakes, puddings, tarts and several other delights on order.*

Baking the Right Entrepreneurial Recipe

Sugar Sisters by *Shemayel & Shurouck*

Finding something to do in life is a necessity. Finding something you love in life is good fortune. And to be able to pursue that you have been granted as a fortune is a luxury. Those who are mindful of this necessity, fortune and luxury are the ones who not only continue on the path of success with their ingenuity and hard work, but are also significantly blessed by the universe in their journey. If you are one of those choicest few, or if you know someone who lives that kind of life, you would know that the aura around this life is something else, something special that makes it stand out and higher than common lives. The sad part is that there is a huge disparity between the people on top of the mountains of success and those at the bottom, staring up above. It isn't that successful people in this world are always born with silver spoons. Neither is it a complete truth that people are born to be successful. If you flip through the pages of world history, you will see that it wasn't those that were made of gold who shone the brightest, but those who toiled hard and shone through the test of endeavours. Instead of sitting either with satiation or resignation, when one takes control of one's fate and discovers what they are truly meant to do with their lives, you have a genius. Haven't you often found yourself being amazed by someone who you knew from work, or who lived next door or had once been your classmate? That someone seemed to live an ordinary life but had somehow managed to turn fate around and taken an extraordinary road. Seems bewildering, doesn't it?

Bewilderment struck me too when I suddenly started hearing news floating all the way from the city of Calicut down from the southern part of the country about two sisters who had created a stir with something incredible. While the media has been talking about them every now and then, it is the number of people who have been impressed and inspired by the siblings that really caught my attention and I set out to explore what has become an incredible example of sibling entrepreneurship in the country.

Shemayel Saleem and Shurouck Saleem are two souls who have grown up together and seen each other through toddlerhood to their teenage years and now as young adults. Having shared the same passion and interests since childhood, the sisters have been the birds of a feather. Growing up has brought them to blend with a series of experiences and developments that have helped them both grow both as individuals as well as siblings. Shemayel as a grown adult, pursued her Bachelor's degree in Business Administration. Exploring her taste buds had always been her hobby and even as a kid, Shemayel was often found savoring delicacies, flirting with flavors and trying out as many cuisines as she could find access to. A simple girl with fun spelling out as her middle name, Shemayel has been a huge fan of shopping and very firmly believes in keeping her family before and beyond anything else in life.

"Even as a teenager, I didn't know where my life was headed but I was extremely clear on the fact that my family is my guiding light through all of my journeys. My sister, in particular, has been my pillar of support. Quite frankly, I don't see myself in any other place than I am in life right now!" Shemayel exclaims with honesty.

The sister she adores and cares for without boundaries is her soulmate Shurouck Saleem. Passionate, sensitive and just as loving as her sister, Shurouck has a life of her own which revolves around mysteries, dynamism and creativity. Unlike her sister, Shurouck is more of a cocktail of everything. In terms of education, she may have completed her course in Bachelors of Economics but in the world of skills and evolution, she is in the continuum of acquiring more interests every day and building her creative expressions in art, design, and culinary forms just to name a few.

This mix and match combination of traits between the sisters, their individual and collective strengths and spirit and their special love for food, could revamp their seemingly ordinary lives in such a swanky way, no one would have even remotely guessed!

The foundation of a tree begins from the day a seed falls into the ground, although the world gets to know of its existence only when the shoot has made its presence known from above the ground; it is only the earth that knows and nurtures the genesis and makes it possible for a new life to emerge strongly. Such has also been the case for Shemayel and Shurouck.

"It started for us many years ago. I loved baking cakes and presenting my confectionery experiments to my family. I would try new things and my family would then give me their feedback, generally good feedback, and I would continue with new and improved style of baking," Shemayel recollects.

Shurouck too was always a part of these initial experiences with the family. Such was their passion towards making cakes that the sisters were often found going to different places only to try out different kinds of baked cuisines. They would often be looking up recipes and videos on the internet, not limiting their exposure to their geographical access of confectionery items. As a result, the sisters were making the best kind of cakes with stunning presentations and creative styles – something one only sees by the hands of trained and professional baking experts. The siblings began to be known by friends and family, and even in the neighborhood as the sisters who baked magic out of sugar. The idea just stuck on from there.

"We realized that since we were anyway dedicating so much of our time and attention to baking cakes out of the sheer love for it, and since this was complimented by approval and appreciation from people, it would be a shame to let this opportunity pass that God had bestowed upon us," Shurouck explains.

It is fascinating how such a simple fact could have grown on to become the true calling for the siblings. Many people in this world find passions in different things – cooking, stitching, planting or painting. And yet, while most let these interests germinate only as hobbies, and very few people dare to pick these blessings and turn them into their livelihoods. This is the singular difference between the ordinary and extraordinary lives; the decision to decide what to do when opportunity knocks at their door!

Destiny, by the time the sisters got into college, was knocking most evidently and promisingly for them and it is then that they opened this door of opportunity and decided to convert their passion into a profession.

"With due advice from family and friends, we began with the idea of opening a bakery store to pour our love and skills of cake making for the world," Shemayal shimmers, "and thus, SugarSisters was born!" From there on, the sisters broke down their requirements and assets to the basics and built up their brand

and product together with a blanket of love and support offered to them by their family.

"It is funny if we think about it now, but back then, the decision to launch SugarSisters had seemed the easiest of what later became an entire rally of critical and difficult decisions for us to make!" they confess. From finding the right place to operate, to building a collection of the right equipment they would need as professional bakers; the needs were endless.

"As people who love baking cakes, we knew that the product side of our business was sorted. But it was the business side of our product that got us to brainstorm immensely," they add. However, Shemayel's education in business administration and Shurouck's passion to not stop at anything short of perfection eventually paid off. And before the sisters had the time to breathe, they had already launched a fully functional brand and begun with their social media advertisements and branding for the world to know what the SugarSisters were baking for it.

"We started getting queries and orders from the moment we launched. So I can't say that we had to face the initial struggle of a slow business or even face the challenge of lack of confidence. SugarSisters had hit if off from day one!" Shemayel cheers.

However, this does not mean that hardships did not come their way and tumble their culinary world.

"You see we had started with the brand while we were still in college. And no matter how strong was our passion for our enterprise, equally important was the pursuit of our education. This was also the will and advice of our family and we couldn't agree more!" they share with seriousness.

Hence, the juggle between classes and baking, assignments and consignments, orders and exams began. "Sometimes we would be at the peak of festive seasons and the phone wouldn't stop ringing for orders while Shemayel and I would be busy trying to adjust between studying and baking cakes!" Shurouck remembers bedazzled.

It was during this true test of temperament and faith that the sisters had the chance of turning either way through their struggle. And I am not surprised to know that they decided they would only head one way, that is to the road of success.

"We have been very lucky in that manner. Whenever there were times when we thought we were losing our heads or beginning to doubt whether we would scrape through any particular order, our mother stood by us with diligent support and encouragement," the sisters speak with gratitude. Their mother not only acted as an earnest pillar of support for her daughters but also stepped in to take care of the administrative roles to make room for her daughters to focus on their education as well as to smoothen the process from baking to delivering at SugarSisters. Even today, sitting at the store, watching the sisters walk and talk as they go about their business, I steal a quick glance at the desk where the mother is sitting, micro-managing some orders and smiling vibrantly through the chaos. I can tell that the apples haven't fallen far from the tree and it is this genetic passion that must have sprouted from the elder generation and blossomed beautifully in the progenies as a result of which we see SugarSisters climbing the stairs of success so gracefully.

I know of many entrepreneurs who do not like to mix their personal and professional lives, or mix family with work. And I have to admit that they are right in that aspiration. However, when I witnessed what happens at this enterprise, I was humbled into changing my opinion. When I asked Shemayel about the number of people she has hired to help the business grow, she gave me a warm smile.

"Everybody you see around here is family. Sometimes, when the pressure is too much, our cousins come down to help us. Some family members even help us to deliver our orders. Have I said this enough number of times that we are very lucky?" She jokes. And yet, in the warmth of her smile, in the happy chit-chats and jokes that the sisters are sharing with all the other members of this family, I can sense what makes SugarSisters stand out from any other cake factory I have ever been to. It's the love, dedication and support system that culminates its warmth and essence into each cake and reveals itself in the stunning silence of pleasure anytime someone takes a bite into those scrumptious delicacies.

"We're family," Shurouck adds simply, "from bits to bounds. Even our funding was generously managed by our father who has wisely set up the stepping stones of SugarSisters."

How apt is the name 'SugarSisters' as I watch the sisters at work in front of my eyes!' I think in my head. The sisters, who mean the world to each other, sweat and serve to bring about this sweet feeling of happiness, only doubly enhanced by the choicest flavors of the cake they bake. "You know, the name for our brand came so naturally to us, it actually amazes me," Shemayel shares. I am amazed too! The sisters, from the beginning of the idea wanted to depict their brand in a manner that reflected the bond of the siblings and at the same time reveal what they were dealing with. I say they couldn't have gotten a name more appropriate!

From juggling through the toughest of times, to actually taking up more endeavours for the benefit of the venture, the sisters have dared and earned. Shurouck in fact went ahead and took a diploma course in baking and culinary arts to polish her skills with the professional nuances to give the brand an edge in their knowledge. However, with the kind of passion and dedication that the duo has for their livelihood stands to me beyond any necessity of degrees or professional training because they seem to have already cracked the best recipe – love! It is this simplicity that has brought success for the SugarSisters in leaps and bounds. In the short period of four years of their being operational, the pair has already acquired a fan base in and around the city that marks them high on the pedestal as compared to the other competitors. What comes as the biggest sign of their success is an entire feature on television that covered their success story on national television. Not only has this worked wonders for their business development and brought in high scale opportunity and exposure but also been a huge morale booster for the duo.

"To see the kind of response we receive in different forms of media and the way people reach out to us after receiving our cakes reveals so much love that it is overwhelming. It makes us feel and be confident that we are definitely on the right track!" they say.

With deliberation and dedication, balance and bounty, the sisters have experienced and evolved not only their personal and professional strengths but explored new bounds of their mutual equation.

"Through this enterprise, we have learned to respect and appreciate each other even more," Shemayel explains, "because it is during the tough times that you truly get to test the strengths of a bond. As it turns out, ours is stronger than steel!" Sharing their responsibilities and work pressure, the sisters have not only perfected the recipe of mouth-watering cakes but also mastered the ingredients of a healthy and happy bond that they mutually enjoy. Once you have set the sky as your limit, it becomes impossible to stop at anything else. As the sisters pace ahead in their endeavour and passion for what they have discovered as their necessity, fortune and privilege, they are building a wave of inspiration around for many more women and especially siblings to find their own calling, to build the courage to pursue their calling and to find support in their siblings for making dreams come true – a delicious concoction indeed!

For your sweet tooth cravings and innovative baking surprises, get in touch with the Sugar Sisters at Facebook:/ sugarsisters4u.

Abhishek *(right) and* **Nishek** *(left) stress on the need of effective language and communication skills through* **VoLT (Vocabulary Learning Techniques)**, *launched first as a published book and now also as a phone-based application.*

The High-VoLTage Brothers

VoLT (Vocabulary Learning Techniques)
by Abhishek & Nishek

As children, we fight with our brothers and sisters all the time. Sometimes, it takes big or small issues to get us triggered against each other, sometimes, it takes none. There is always something one does or has or says that annoys the other and an endless battle begins with no conclusive result, only recurring trouble for the ordained parents. However, if the same set of siblings are projected against a third agent of disruption, the forces of the siblings unite against all odds and fight any external trouble – whether it is the next door neighbor's dog, bullies from school or a random stranger at the mall who acts too friendly for comfort. It is in the face of such circumstances, that the brotherhood unites and faces the enemy while watching each other's backs.

Adulthood is not very different. Siblings, that have grown up with the same challenges, fears, strengths and understanding, also deal with the enemies of adult life in a similar fashion. They have each other's back, fend for each other, support each other and battle through the worst together. Sometimes these enemies are people, but many times, these enemies are figurative –

circumstances, weaknesses or situations posed before us that we may not be best prepared for. However, to know that someone is watching out for us, unconditionally and selflessly, is more than a relief – it is a source of encouragement to embrace life with its challenges.

When small town boys Abhishek and Nishek ventured out into the big world of big cities in the country, their eyes filled with dreams and the passion to make the best of their lives, they were served with lemons!

"We went through the same challenge that any young beginner from a small town experiences when they step into the fast paced and competitive environment," Abhishek, the elder of the two siblings begins to explain the situation in retrospection. Despite being equally skilled and knowledgeable as engineering students, both Abhishek and Nishek faced the challenge of expressing themselves confidently in the English language that happens to be the language in which major formal communication in the country is done, especially in the field of education. "We found ourselves to be at the other end of the spectrum when it came to effective communication in English, and this was turning into a major factor that was pushing us back in all aspects," Nishek, the younger sibling confirms his brother's statement. Like hundreds and thousands of other such students or young professionals who migrate every year from the colloquial comforts of small towns into the aggressive pursuits of big cities, the brothers also struggled through their education period by making efforts to strengthen their hold on the English language.

"We tried reading articles in good newspapers, magazines or watching documentary films to get a grasp of the language," Nishek explains the earlier predicament. However, a common shortcoming of this practice is that it doesn't help in consistent development of the vocabulary – at least not in an organized and progressive way.

"Abhishek and I would often discuss this issue and keep prodding over a solution for this," he recollects.

Sometimes innovation comes out of necessity and sometimes, opportunities bring out innovation. More often than not these opportunities come out of the environment one is exposed to. While studying in premier institutes has brought its share of pressure and challenges for both the brothers, it has also brought them the opportunity to be exposed to brilliant knowledge and information. It was during the second year of his engineering when Abhishek undertook an optional psychology course. It here that he was first introduced to the concept of learning with associations. This experience changed his perspective about acquiring information altogether.

"When we generally get stuck with a new word while reading something, our immediate response is to look it up in the dictionary and try to grasp its meaning. However, it was a repetitive problem that both Nishek and I were facing that the very next time we would come across that word, we would have forgotten the word's meaning completely."

Abhishek highlights the root of the concept he later developed for a productive cause. But the concept of association of words with images, beautiful pictures to create long-lasting memory was something that the young engineer found peculiarly fascinating. Not only did he experiment with the principle to increase his vocabulary, but also introduced Nishek to the idea and soon, the brothers started realizing that the concept could be used massively to strengthen their vocabulary, and consequently, their command over the English language.

It was then, after having experimented and learned from the concept themselves that Abhishek and Nishek decided to write their own book and publish it as their own publishing house to propagate and encourage the idea of building vocabulary with association.

"We decided to set up our own publishing house – RR Publications – and published the book, *VoLT – Vocabulary Learning Techniques*, in January 2013 and it sold over 10,000 copies," Abhishek speaks with pride. It was an idea and implementation that became an instant hit since the brothers had caught the nerve of thousands of struggling people who could now avail the concept and battle the language barrier. The book instantly became one of the top 10 vocabulary books on Flipkart and Amazon.

However, this was only a milestone that got the siblings inspired to expand the outreach of VoLT to an even larger audience, with more efficiency.

"After a point, we realized that although the book was being very well-received by readers, we were getting constant requests through emails and letters to publish a second part of the book," Nishek explains. While it was a clear signal that VoLT was doing its magic and effectively helping the target audience with the problem of vocabulary enhancement in English, there was more to the story.

"It's true that the book had helped people, but it is also true that a particular book only holds a limited number of words that cannot be replaced. Equally fair is the interpretation that the reach of our book was limited to a specific number of people, owing to affordability and ease of access," reflects Abhishek. It was with this realization that the brothers decided to enhance the concept of VoLT to present it in a version that could touch and change many lives with ease. Technology served to be their modus operandi in this mission and thus, with a lot of deliberation and brainstorming, Abhishek and Nishek were able to build an exclusive android based application with its original name VoLT in 2016.

"With the help of this app we can add as many words as we want (or people demand) and also our work is now available to a much larger population (anyone having an android smart phone) and that too absolutely free," explains the older innovator.

As a senior faculty member in one of the most prestigious entities of the country with seven years of experience to his credit, Abhishek has been well-known and loved for his innovative methods of teaching by his students and colleagues alike. Nishek, on the other hand, has had a plethora of experience through his education and work, both in and outside of the country along with his achievement of cracking the examination for IES.

"Every year, an unimaginable number of candidates from small towns and cities struggle to crack some of the most difficult competitive examinations of the country like UPSC, SSC, Bank PO, CAT, GRE, GMAT etc. Despite being very skilled and capable of cracking several aspects of these examinations, a lot of these candidates struggle hard to cram words of the English language with hopes of scoring the bare minimum necessary in such exams," Nishek explains, "But ever since the launch of VoLT, thousands of these people are finding this app very helpful because now they are able to not only remember all these words in a very fun and fast way but also retain the meanings and the usage in their minds for a much longer duration."

It is no surprise then that within merely two months of its launch, VoLT has already achieved more than twenty five thousand downloads. The product has been receiving excellent feedback and has been critically acclaimed by educationists and innovators alike.

Behind this array of acclamations and popularity lies a series of struggles that have gotten the brothers strong and consistent with their innovation.

"To understand and accept your own weakness is the first step towards success. The second step, of course, is to work towards turning this very weakness into a drive of finding strength," Abhishek shares insightfully. This is exactly what the brothers went through while strengthening their own hold on the language, uplifting their own confidence and consequently working on projecting this achievement towards the benefit of others. However, with no external funders or investors, the brothers had to burn their own savings at a stage which would make or break their innovative venture. While facing the financial challenge, another area of difficulty for the brothers has been building a reliable team that can relate to their vision, understand their perspective and bring in dedicated energy in sync with their innovation. While the advent of the product had been to test the concept and make it accessible to people who most needed the aid of VoLT, the brothers are now working on a business revenue model. Taking this as a venture with constant growth and improvement, both Abhishek and Nishek try to bring in the best of their talents to the table.

It is not that this dynamic duo has been venturing together only along their entrepreneurial journey. This equation has metamorphosed into a deeper connection where the best and worst of the siblings come to play with each other.

"We have grown up fighting the same battles and we know how to handle situations whether they are related to things between us, or against any external factor," Nishek smiles confidently.

While working on their creation, the brothers have explored their skills and areas of interest, putting them to use for VoLT. With their roles defined in the professional equation, the brothers maintain a balance between mutual cooperation and individual instinctiveness. While Abhishek handles Content Creation, Business Development, Team Building for the enterprise, Nishek's responsibilities include Marketing and Operations. With their experience and domains of expertise, the brothers spend their days endeavouring to enhance their personal skills. Not only are they supported by the presence and blessings of very encouraging parents but also supported by Abhishek's wife Smita, initially as a source of guidance, and eventually as a full-fledged participation in the form of their chief financial officer. With such a reliable and ubiquitous set of minds at work, the adventure of VoLT not only excites the brothers to work harder, but also, inevitably bears fruitful results.

With results to their credit and each other's support, Abhishek and Nishek have been working on expansion and escalation plans for VoLT. Having started out to share personal experience and resolve a common problem of their target audience, they now feel inspired to resolve similar problems and broaden the horizon of services than being currently provided by VoLT.

"I can't say that we have been a hundred percent successful but yes, to see people's response and the significant changes we have been able to bring in their lives is definitely a motivation to take things forward." Abhishek describes their ultimate aim as "making VoLT a one stop solution for all the English language related problems of Indians." And the way things seem to be headed, it does not seem like a far off ambition. With such milestones to their credit, it makes one wonder about the recipe that has helped them come this far.

"I think it makes a big difference that Abhishek is here to walk with me through this journey; I couldn't have found a better partner, friend or guide to work with," Nishek speaks with no uncertain reflection of gratitude. With the same roots, values, problems and strengths at hand, it is obvious that the siblings find deep connection and confirmation in each other's presence. Whether you witness it in the amount of attention and advice sought by the brothers from their parents, or find the presence of the parents and the grandparents at the launch of the book that started this journey many years ago, a known and well-felt presence of family's collective responsibility towards each other's well-being shows the depth of the sibling's relationship.

What started out as inference of a common knowledge, transformed into a personal experience that the brothers shared to solve their mutual problem. That, one may say, is not so uncommon in siblings or even friends. But to convert this knowledge and experience into a substantial development that eventually led to the betterment of a much larger good, is not so commonplace. It takes a certain degree of conviction, hard-work, and above all, a desire to turn the tables around to transform a challenge into an opportunity is what one learns from the story of this innovative pair of brothers. With VoLT, both Abhishek and Nishek have been generating and radiating extraordinary energy and productive consequences for people who may not have found such an efficient and accessible solution for such a widespread problem. With sheer brilliance, the brothers have humbly set forth an example of true bonding and understanding towards each other that has led to astonishing achievements.

 You can download the VoLT App from the Play Store or grab a copy of the bestselling book.

WittyFeed *was engineered with precision and nurtured with love by* **Parveen** *(left),* **Vinay** *(middle) and* **Shashank** *(right), aiming to give the world the best of stories and videos to enjoy.*

A Brother by Birth and a Brother by Bond

WittyFeed by Vinay, Shashank & Parveen

So many sleepless nights have been spent in hostel rooms, with youthful dreams and ambitious plans. Many ideas are born and built, some die on the other side of the sleep. Some live to see the morning of fond memories. Some even become half way milestones for the daring few who take the brain storming day-dreaming sessions to the next level. But it is this undisputed golden period of bricking aspirations with the cement of potential that becomes the foundation of creating dynamic adults out of college boys. Some use this period to sail through the tough years of education by fitting into suitable company of peers, some step up further still and discover friendship that becomes more meaningful than most bonds they have had for life. It is out of these bonds, companionships and explorations of equations that the lucky few also find people who grow up to become their brother from another mother. Such bonds stand strong through the test of time and such friendships culminate into bonding that spills beyond coffee table discussions or night outs. These are the people who practically become the pillars of each other's life.

Exploring such bonds of brotherhood and friendship, I walked into the swankiest of offices in the city of Indore; a place that the entire internet is crazy about, one that churns more creative juices than probably a buffet of artists would have in the streets of Italy during the Renaissance movement. With colors to break clutter, triggers to instigate brain-storming and seats to put you into a comfortable, playful mood, it took some effort to shut my awestruck jaw. While some places were filled with people diligently chalking ideas on boards, others were surprisingly calm and soothing. It was in this corner that I saw someone with his head on the ground and feet up in the air – the Sirshasan posture. "Brain-storming has many meanings. This is me storming my brain with blood-flow and energy. That's how most of my ideas are born!"

Meet the young and very talented Shashank Vaishnav who can charm you with a smile and engage you in a relay of conversations that will blow your mind. Shashank, at twenty-six, is one of the most dynamic leaders, a masterly thinker, a creative simulator and co-founder of the second most successful content generation portal in its domain in the entire world! He is also a friend, partner and brother by bond to his best-friend from college and his comrade for both personal and professional journeys. Vinay Singhal, the other co-founder in the picture, was also the founder of dreams with Shashank back in their days in engineering college. The first member in his family to dream big and pursue engineering, Vinay is known for his perfection, for his die hard attitude and for his larger than life energy that puts a zing on anything it touches.

A small hostel room in Chennai witnessed the formulation of ideas and action plans that culminated into many entrepreneurial endeavours, ventures, failures and successes initiated by the ambitious pair. With serious deliberation, this pursuit led to the establishment of Vatsana Technologies in 2011. Times changed, other founding members altered their aspirations too, but before and beyond everything, Vatsana stayed afloat and sailed through many days of crests and troughs. With their independent as well as mutual interests and capacities, the duo had an array of skill sets including content development, social media management, business strategy to name a few from the list. How this buffet grew into a mammoth business is a story straight out what would make a great film script! It all started with a page on Facebook where they would put together things of interest that people would like to read and engage with.

"With a whooping four million followers of the page, we realized that it was time for us to monetize this audience. So we built a website and put ad sense and started our journey. Later we realized that it was a common problem. A lot of other pages had an audience, but no content, and that is why we came up with the idea of starting a platform that would have content in a myriad of categories," Vinay explains about the genesis.

In September 2014, the dynamic duo launched WittyFeed as a solution which is a one stop platform for content creators, consumers, and publishers. Declaring it as the 'Mecca of virality,' the co-founders explain the enterprise as being a modern age tool for all mediums of expression that is redefining how the internet can access and generate content.

However, the stalwarts of this viral genius were not born with silver spoons or lucky charms. In fact, it was each other's support, their true brilliance and the drive to excel, no matter what that changed their course of growth. A little sneak peek into what went behind the making of what we know as WittyFeed today is a spellbinding story. After Vatsana Technologies launched into the world of enterprises, many hurdles of time, financial investment, stress of academic pursuit for the college students and change in priorities came to action. While most members and friends drifted apart, Shashank and Vinay continued their efforts.

"It was at this stage that we walked on different roads for about a year, making our own discoveries, building our own strengths," Shashank recollects.

'These are the best of times, these are the worst of times' was certainly true for the friends as well as brothers! Despite their individual accomplishments during their time away from each other, the duo found themselves at a juncture that shook them up.

"Just when we thought we had hit the right spots in our respective work, my mentor turned his back on me. Exactly around this time, Shashank was on the verge of signing the most devastating of deals had it come through!" Vinay expresses with an obvious relief in his tone about what happened next.

This jolt, that actually came as a blessing in disguise for the duo, brought them back together as they planned to merge the best of their endeavours. Thus, with a series of failures, dead ends and bankruptcies to their list of incredible experiences, Shashank and Vinay got back together to build WittyFeed and bring it into what has today become the largest website in the country in terms of content generation and amongst the top 25 most read websites in the UK.

While these brothers from different mothers were exploring and earning credits in the world of enterprise, there was another person, close to both Shashank and Vinay, equally passionate about the charisma of the internet. This was the then seventeen-year-old brother of Vinay, Parveen. It was Parveen who had discovered and started tapping on the phenomenon of internet virality and mastered its tricks and treats. Today, as the third co-founder of

WittyFeed and a dedicated power-house COO, he is the man who takes care of the social media, content, and traffic acquisition for the venture and at twenty-one, stands suavely as one of the youngest successful entrepreneurs of the country. Thus, the brothers cum friends cum entrepreneurs form the most invincible trio that is breaking hell loose on internet with their wit, sharpness, strategy and determination.

Sitting in the office buzzing with energy, enthusiasm and evidently pouring success, you wonder what at all would be missing, or even remotely challenging for this trio who seem to have cracked the code! But a simple question to the co-founders will bring you the answer, bringing along with it an astounding insight into how simple and yet supreme effects do experiences and especially failures have in the lives of great men.

"You have to go through the failures and mishaps to understand what works and what doesn't," Shashank explains. "And I consider us very lucky to have figured out at least what doesn't work."

In the beginning of their experiments with the venture, Shashank and Vinay indulged in what they call parallel entrepreneurship, investing in many ideas around web content and more. While these experiments were individually doing fairly well, the co-founders soon realized that it was diverting and distracting their resources into way too many channels.

"There came a stage when we had more content and users on our portals than needed. This could have been a time to sail away in the flow and let the many streams of Vatsana overwhelm us," Vinay shares, "but we took this time to step out into an objective purview and look at where we wanted to head and how we wanted to steer this now giant ship."

With great power comes great money – the trio at WittyFeed had already witnessed this within the first few years of operation.

But it was time to endorse even greater responsibility instead of simply being a ruthless money churning organization with their heads diverted in many directions.

"At this point, we had to make some serious decisions. You see, every idea that we have metamorphosed into a business action has been like our little baby, with its brilliance, appropriateness and the sheer amount of input that has gone into the making, it is heart breaking to have to pull the plug on those ideas," Shashank shares candidly.

However, for the sake of the big dream, smaller ideas have to be looked over and this is exactly what the co-founders did. This led to the painful yet necessary withdrawal of all other verticals of Vatsana Technologies and pooling all resources and focus behind WittyFeed. And it turned out, as it does in decisions of the most intellectually sound people of the world, WittyFeed started churning faster and higher results in terms of usership, performance and revenue generation. Within just under a couple of years of operation, the incredibly unique and efficient enterprise has already become a beast generating more than sixty stories every day, a traffic of seventy-five million unique visitors every month, profits of unimaginable demeanor and writer base of more than a hundred people.

"These are not just numbers that look good in presentations. These are actual reflections on the number of lives we touch in every form, every single day with quality content coming to us from different parts of the world, reaching different parts of the world," says Vinay, a social activist at heart.

While it may be this level achievement that impresses you about the young entrepreneurial trio that has broken trends and set benchmarks for the world of start-ups in this country to envy and draw inspiration from, it is actually the disposition of these self-made men, despite their position that is truly mind-boggling.

To say the least, these stalwarts are humble. Staring at the sheer magnanimity of WittyFeed, and this includes not only their swanky office space with an impressive score full of talented employees but also the various Google searches that reveal a high success quotient of the venture, pride is well-earned. And yet, when you ask them about what they attribute this immaculate success to, the response comes with an earnest smile,

"It is this masterly team that we have been blessed to find. They drive us, trigger us, endure us and inspire us. I think we're just a bunch of ideas; they're the machinery that convert these ideas to reality," Vinay humbly praises the team.

The world around him knows his philanthropy, patience and the quality to look at the best in people. It is perhaps this asset that has helped him partner up with his brother and friend so amicably and also granted him the privilege of bringing out the best in people he works with. It is also the undying spirit despite failures and challenges that allows for the witty trio to appreciate everything they have and to bring them to such a grounded stance despite all achievements.

Watching them float around from one team to another, from calls to meetings, I wonder what their life would be outside of these work walls.

"It's the same," Parveen responds with a knowing grin, "We are here at nine in the morning and stay till past midnight. This is life, this is work, this is passion and this is pursuit."

A simple declaration from the young man is enough to tell you that the trio feel no boundaries that compartmentalize their life from their livelihood.

"Some people call it the burden of being an entrepreneur. I call it the perks of being one!" Shashank adds. With little time at hand for any engagements apart from WittyFeed, they try to indulge in little hobbies like working out, surfing the net for the latest bikes or simply keeping themselves updated with the happenings of the world. Things back home can be challenging for them, one can assume, but even in this diocese, they have mastered the power of words to find their way through!

"Back in the days while we were completing our graduation, we did not sit for any placements and were hell bent on building our own enterprise," Vinay recollects. "This obviously did not go down well with our parents who belong to very a simple, small town, middle class background."

But determination and dexterities are assets that helped the aspiring entrepreneurs to convince even the most traditional mind sets into letting them explore their ambitions.

"You have to see that this is beyond Vinay or Parveen or my own dreams. We are setting into motion a phenomenon that will change the way careers, enterprises and the net-kingdom is perceived by the common man in this country," Shashank declares.

In this task, they have now earned the support of many believers, contributors, family members and stake holders who have shown confidence in this spirit of the trio. "I am lucky to have a wife and colleague who not only understand and appreciate my passion, despite the test it puts our personal time through, but also contributes as valued member of the team of WittyFeed and stands by me no matter what," Vinay speaks fondly of Ananya, his better half.

These bonds and brotherhood, failures and fights, struggles and success, experiences and exertions are all parts of this incredible story of the high and low journey that Vinay, Shashank and Parveen have undertaken through all these years. By dividing work domains, areas of expertise and responsibilities, they have sensibly learned to keep conflicts at bay and to blend into each other's style of working. While the two elders of the trio have brought perspectives, experiences and insight to this table of partnership, Parveen, by virtue of his sharp understanding of social media has brought in a fresh perspective and diligence to become the 'Viral King' of the enterprise. A true ambience of mutual respect, appreciation and faith radiates through the vibrant walls of the WittyFeed office. With diverse opinions and powerful decisions, with inclusive brain storming and individual chiseling, some days at WittyFeed end with cheers and some with decisions that may not find unanimous agreement. However, as Vinay puts it honestly,

"All days end with a hug or a handshake no matter what. That is what keeps us strong together." Inspiring generations, building trends and beating benchmarks of excellence set by global stalwarts, the trio are all set with their focus on becoming the top domain for content generation in the world. Not only do they go on to prove that one does not need a cushioned environment or a conducive background to make it big in any enterprise, but that daring to dream and driving to make that dream come true is what it takes to make people even from the humblest backgrounds into the leaders influencing stories of the world. The trio has proved their equation to be purer than the bonds of blood, stronger than the connections of DNA. Reasserting their intentions of doing good and doing it in the best way possible, they certainly are feeding the world with their wit and the same energy that had initiated its form many years ago in a hostel room in Chennai. Here's to making dreams come true.

To read and watch some interesting stories, visit www.wittyfeed.com or follow them on Facebook: / wittyfeed.

By the same author

Superwomen: Inspiring stories of 20 women entrepreneurs

In a nation that reveres women as goddesses of wealth, knowledge, power and infinite energy, there are a few who have gone on to prove why. Not only have they carved a niche for their talent, but have also inspired and empowered many others in the process.

Superwomen is an interesting journey of how these twenty women entrepreneurs played all their roles to perfection, aligning their families with their ambitions, showing the world their true mettle.

SuperCouples: Inspiring stories of couple-preneurs

Rather than searching for a partner for their enterprise outside, real life couples in relationships have started exploring the idea of partnering up in business too!

SuperCouples brings out stories of enterprising couples whose dynamic startups break stereotypes and cover a varied range of services.